Deena took a deep breath and looked around the room, at each one of her teammates. "I'm sorry," she began. "I'm sorry I wasn't there last weekend. I'm so sorry I let everyone down. I should have talked with everyone, but I just couldn't."

She stopped here. Maybe she didn't want to say this out loud. It would be so real if she said it out loud. But it *was* real.

"My dad is sick," she said, making eye contact with Mr. Humphries for reassurance. He nodded. . . .

Carly, sitting next to her, put an arm around Deena's shoulder and pulled her close. "We had no idea," she whispered. She looked around at everyone else, hoping they would help her in this moment. "It's OK, girl," she continued. "We got your back. I promise."

Second Wind

KATE FAGAN

Second Wind

TP **THE TOWNSEND LIBRARY**

For more titles in the Townsend Library,
visit our website: **www.townsendpress.com**

Copyright © 2012 by Townsend Press, Inc.
Printed in the United States of America

9 8 7 6 5 4 3 2 1

Cover illustration © 2012 by Hal Taylor

Townsend Press, Inc.
439 Kelley Drive
West Berlin, NJ 08091
permissions@townsendpress.com

ISBN-13: 978-1-59194-293-1
ISBN-10: 1-59194-293-4

Library of Congress Control Number:
2012932127

Chapter 1

Deena pretended not to hear her mother's call to dinner. She was tucked into the overstuffed chair in the corner of her room, her nose buried in a book. Happily absorbed by the story, she did not have to think of the unhappiness in her own life.

Only one chapter left. She turned the book sideways to see how many pages. Not more than 15 minutes of reading.

"Deena!" came her mother's second call, closer now. "I said dinner's ready!"

Deena sighed. She placed her bookmark at the start of the last chapter and stood. Her long legs, growing daily, seemed like stilts. She stood, towering over the corner chair, as her mother pushed open the door.

"You're still in here?" Her mother acted annoyed, but Deena knew she wasn't. "Aren't you done with that book *yet*?"

"One more chapter."

"Well, it's going to have to wait. Dinner is ready."

"I heard something about that," Deena said, smiling. "Can I bring my book to the table?"

"Honey . . ."

"Okay, okay," Deena said, dropping the book onto the chair. "I'll wait until after." She followed her mother to the kitchen. Her father, Wilson, and her brother, Jamal, were already seated.

"Nice of you to join us," said her father.

Deena and her mother slipped into their seats, and the four of them joined hands. A second later, the room was filled with her father's voice, blessing the steaming food.

Dad was a burly man, mostly muscle. He'd never gone to college, but started as a construction worker, years ago. His company became so impressed with him that he was promoted to assistant foreman. It was a tiring job, often with long hours, but he was able to pull his family from a run-down rental into this in-between neighborhood. Their street, with its ranch-style brick houses, was adjacent to Philadelphia's Fairmount Park. It was one of the safer streets in the neighborhood, although Deena knew never to go into the park at night.

Neither of Deena's parents had attended college, but they'd always told Deena that she would be different.

"Amen," concluded her father, reaching for his fork. "This looks wonderful, Candice." He smiled at his wife.

"Looks can be deceiving," she said, and then turned her attention to Deena and Jamal. "Don't ignore your broccoli."

Jamal, who looked so small sitting next to his father, speared a piece with his fork and popped it into his mouth. He put a wide grin on his face. "Mmmm," he said, swallowing dramatically. "So good."

Deena laughed, which caused her mom to flash a disapproving look.

"So what does the school week look like for you guys?" said her father, his mouth full.

Deena looked down at her plate. She pushed the broccoli from one side to the other and hoped her brother would fill the silence for both of them. Underneath the table, her mom squeezed her knee reassuringly.

Jamal, the star of his eighth grade class, began reeling off that week's schedule: a school assembly on Tuesday, a baseball game on Thursday, and an end-of-year field trip on Friday. Jamal adored school. And why shouldn't he? Everyone wanted to be his friend.

Deena watched Jamal talk. He was so enthusiastic and engaging. He was genuinely excited about the upcoming school week.

On the other hand, Deena couldn't wait for the week to be over. Summer started next week. For three months, she wouldn't be the un-cool kid. She wouldn't be the one who sat at the un-cool table during lunch, struggled to find a partner for the biology project, or wasn't chosen as a teammate during gym class.

Her father turned his attention toward her. "And what about you, sweetie?"

Why does he always do this? Deena thought, her frustration rising. *It just makes everything so much worse.*

"I don't know, Dad." Deena met his gaze. "Same as every week, I guess."

"So you're looking forward to summer?"

"I'm just trying to make it to summer, actually." Deena filled her mouth with broccoli so she wouldn't be able to say anything mean.

She chewed it slowly.

"Don't let things hold you back, baby girl," said her dad, sensing his daughter's anxiety. "You're a star."

Deena, her cheeks filled, smiled weakly at him. She thought of a moment during last week's gym class.

Deena had gym during the middle of the day, just before lunch, and she always changed into her clothes in a corner of the locker room where no one else stood. She turned her back to the other girls and slipped into her white t-shirt and black gym shorts.

A few girls were already heading out to the gymnasium, so Deena fell into line behind them, careful not to make it seem as if she was joining their group. They pushed through the heavy swinging door into the gym. Girls gradually started filling the space, standing in small groups, chatting, and waiting for their teacher's instructions.

Deena spotted an empty seat on the first row of the bleachers. She sat down and waited, smiling at a classmate also sitting alone. Then she heard the shrill sound of the teacher's whistle.

"All right, everyone, quiet down!" Their teacher thundered into the middle of the gym, a bag of volleyballs slung over her shoulder. It was only then that Deena noticed the net set up on the right half of the gym.

"We're starting our volleyball unit today," the teacher continued. "Let me see hands for volunteers: Who wants to be a team captain?"

Deena's heart began beating rapidly. She hated this tactic, this popularity contest. It was a brutal public display of who would be the first chosen, and who would be the last. She stared down at the tops of her shoes and listened while the teacher chose two names she recognized: Carly and Monique. They were the two best athletes in the class, always the first to volunteer for any challenge. Deena did not like them or dislike them; she wasn't even sure the two knew she existed.

Deena listened as the first few rounds of players were chosen. She glanced at the girl sitting to her right, and the two of them exchanged a pained look. Finally, Deena stood up and joined the remaining group of girls who had yet to be picked. Maybe joining the crowd would prevent her from being the absolutely last person chosen, merely out of circumstance.

The group around Deena continued thinning out as each chosen girl walked forward and joined either Carly or Monique's team. As each girl walked away, Deena's embarrassment rose. Finally, she was the only one standing there, except for the girl from the bleachers.

It was Carly's turn to pick. The entire gym glass stared at them. Although Carly's decision felt especially important to Deena—she wanted so badly not to be last—Carly herself did not seem to care much one way or the other.

Deena looked up as Carly raised her finger to point at one of them. She did not seem to know either of their names or, if she did, did not feel particularly compelled to use them.

Carly pointed at the girl to Deena's right. Deena's heart dropped, and her face flushed red. The girl, relieved, walked forward to stand behind Carly.

Deena glanced over at Monique, who'd landed her on her team merely by default. Monique shrugged and said loudly, "Yeah, sure, whatever."

After gym class, Deena had her study period. She walked to the library, pushing through the heavy wooden door in hopes that one of the girls she sat with at lunch—Whitney or Ashley—

would already be in the room, studying. Deena gripped a book in her hand, tucking it under her armpit. Books, as they'd been for years, were her weapons against shyness. She could not be assured, in the library or in the lunchroom, that one of her few friends would also be present, and she could never build up the courage to ask others if she could join them at their table.

Deena looked out across the silent room. To the right of the stacks of books, a few students sat together at circular tables, but she did not see Whitney or Ashley. She walked past the tables, eyes straight ahead, as if she was looking for someone. The library also contained a few chairs behind the book stacks. Sometimes, Deena would sit back here to escape the loneliness of sitting at an empty table. But other students had similar thoughts, and these chairs were almost always taken.

She turned the corner around the last stack. All of the chairs were filled. One of the students, a girl Deena believed was a sophomore, looked up from her books and smiled softly. She understood.

Walking back to the front the library, Deena lifted her backpack onto one of the circular tables. She slid into the chair and placed the book in front of her. Immediately, without looking at any of her surrounding classmates, she opened the book and began reading.

This way, she hoped, her classmates would assume she was too busy to worry about sitting alone.

Deena had never been popular. She was not disliked, but had always been invisible, partly as a result of her own shyness. When she was in second grade, the eye doctor prescribed thick glasses, and her mom had selected a pair with wide pink frames, the lenses half an inch thick and appearing very similar to goggles. A few years later, she'd endured a growth spurt that made her taller than most of the boys. And after that, she'd been fitted for braces.

Even now, as a junior in high school, Deena was considered a nonentity. She'd had the braces removed her freshman year and had switched to contacts a year after that. None of it seemed to change the image already created in her classmates' minds. She often felt like a ghost in their presence. And she sometimes wanted to call out just to see if anyone was paying attention.

• • •

Deena felt her mother's hand covering her own.

"Wilson," Mom said, "we all know Deena would rather be reading her books than out at all those parties anyway."

"Of course she would," said her father, but neither of them was convinced.

"Thanks, Mom." Deena rolled her eyes.

Deena was certain that if she transferred to a different high school, she'd have a chance to be cool. Her new classmates wouldn't know about the thick glasses, the bulky braces, and the awkward growth spurt. She could present herself exactly as she currently appeared: tall, yes, but not unusually so; contacts hiding her poor eyesight; and straightened teeth from those multi-colored braces.

Sometimes at night, Deena would stand in front of her full-length bedroom mirror and try to look at herself objectively. Was she really that unlikeable? Would it really be that awful to be seen with her?

"Honey," said Deena's mom, snapping her out of her fog, "you can go read your book now, if you'd like."

Deena could see the sympathy in her mom's eyes. "No, that's OK," she said, noticing her plate was still filled with food. "I can read later." She turned to her dad to ask him a question, but his face was contorted with pain. He raised his right hand as if to stop the oncoming question.

"Dad?" she asked, her concern rising.

He slammed his closed fist onto the table. The impact shook the water in each of their glasses. Dad, head down, put a hand to his chest.

"Honey, what is it?" Mom quickly stood up. She pushed back her chair so abruptly that it threatened to tip over behind her. Deena reached over to steady it and then watched her mother as she knelt beside her father. He was shaking his head as if to say it wasn't all right.

"Mom!" Deena's voice was shaking. "What is it? What's happening?"

Deena watched her mom feel for her father's pulse and then place a hand on his forehead. Sweat beads instantly formed on his brow. For a few seconds, she watched her mom, who seemed deep in thought. For the last 17 years, Mom had worked as a nurse, and so Deena imagined the different thoughts now coursing through her mind.

"Mom!" Deena tried again.

"Call an ambulance," said her mom, locking eyes with Deena. "Now."

Deena hesitated, unsure how this moment had come upon them so quickly, but then she raced to the kitchen phone and dialed 911.

Hours later, Deena sat in an uncomfortable hospital chair, her book open on her lap. She'd been staring at the final pages for at least two hours, but she couldn't absorb the words. She and her mother and brother were tucked into a corner of the visitors' center at Hahnemann Hospital, waiting for any word on her father.

Jamal was asleep, his head resting on Deena's shoulder. Her mother was seated next to her, flipping through her third or fourth magazine. Every half hour or so, she'd toss the magazine onto the side table, as if exasperated with its contents. A few minutes later, she'd pick up another one. It was as if her mother wasn't comfortable without some form of distraction.

It was nearing 11 p.m. when a doctor finally approached them. Deena nudged her brother awake. The three of them adjusted themselves in their seats, sitting up straighter. A fan whirled overhead, the only sound between them for a few seconds.

"Mrs. Jackson?" asked the doctor, eyes leveled on her mom.

"Yes . . ."

"Your husband is fine," said the doctor, removing a pen from his coat pocket and fiddling with it. "He suffered a mild heart attack tonight."

Her mother released a long sigh, as if she'd been holding her breath.

The doctor seemed about to continue speaking, but stopped and looked at the three of them. Then he continued, attention back on Mom, "I was hoping you'd join me in your husband's room for a few minutes."

"Yes, of course." Mom stood and trailed the doctor through the swinging doors.

Deena wasn't sure how to feel. She felt relieved that her dad's heart attack had been mild, but something about the doctor's demeanor had left her anxious.

Deena and Jamal waited for an hour before their mother reappeared through the visiting room's doors. She was unaccompanied this time, although she seemed more distant and preoccupied than when she had left. Deena watched her navigate the tables and chairs as she made her way toward them. Mom's eyes were downcast, as if she was following a line drawn along the carpet. Finally, she stood before them and offered a thin smile.

"He's OK?" asked Deena.

"The heart attack was mild, and he's awake right now, in his room."

"So everything is going to be OK?" Deena asked again.

"You'll get to see him very soon."

The thought of seeing her father *very soon* frightened Deena. There were too many unknowns in this hospital, which they'd never before visited. At home, she could picture her dad in so many places he spent time: under the sink fixing the always-breaking garbage disposal, relaxing on his recliner during the football game, helping Jamal with his math homework at the dinner table. But here? She could not picture him here. Trying to do so felt like trying to picture a different father altogether. And who could do that?

Deena looked into her mother's eyes, which seemed closed although they were open. "OK," Deena finally said, standing. She couldn't be scared of seeing her dad, even if he was collapsed on a white hospital bed, trapped inside a disinfected room.

Jamal stood too, and Mom instantly wrapped them in a hug. Deena could feel her short, quick breaths turn into tears, which then turned into heavy, deep breathing. She opened one eye and caught her brother's attention. The two looked at each other for a second until Deena finally lifted her shoulders slightly, conveying the sense of confusion they were both feeling. She shook her head as if to tell her brother she was at a loss, also. They both held onto their mother for a second longer.

"Mom, he's OK, everything is OK," Deena said, peeling herself out of Mom's embrace.

"Yes, of course." Mom straightened her shirt and wiped at her eyes. "Let's go see him."

The three of them tiptoed into the darkened hospital room. All Deena could see were shadows of things: a hospital bed, a dripping IV machine, a wall-mounted television. She'd never seen such things, so they presented themselves almost as if in a dream. The room was filled with the constant beep and hum of machines that seemed, in the darkness, like futuristic monsters.

Her father was asleep. The doctor had said he might be, and not to wake him if he was, because his body needed the sleep. He'd be awake soon enough, the doctor had told them, so be patient.

Deena and Jamal sat in the chairs underneath the television, while their mother pulled a chair next to Dad's bed and gave him a soft kiss on the cheek. He didn't stir.

"Come say hi to your father," Mom whispered.

Jamal glanced at Deena. They both inched over to their father until they were casting their own eerie shadows across his sleeping outline. Deena leaned down and planted a kiss on his forehead. Jamal did the same. This seemed to satisfy their mother.

Suddenly, the door opened, bringing with it the hallway's bright light. A flood of yellow landed on the hospital bed and the family's hovering outlines. "I'm sorry to interrupt," said the doctor they'd all met in the waiting room. "I was just going to check in on our patient."

The doctor stood in the glow of the hallway, shifting his glance between Mom, Deena, and Jamal. He seemed to be looking for an answer to an unknown question. Finally his gaze landed on Mom, and Deena noticed the nearly imperceptible side-to-side movement of her mother's head, no more than a centimeter each way. It seemed to answer whatever question the doctor had silently asked.

"I'll give you guys some more time," he said, backing into the doorway. "Visiting hours are over in 25 minutes, but take as long as you need."

As the doctor disappeared, the door clicked shut. Deena hated sitting in the darkness with all the strange smells and strange shadows. "What was that about?" she asked her mother, with more accusation in her voice than she'd intended. Jamal's eyes lifted, surprised.

"What was what about?" asked Mom, rubbing her hands on her knees as she often did when nervous. Her palms weren't sweaty, but Deena recognized it as her mom's nervous habit. It was as if she could transfer her fear and worry to some other surface.

"Mom," Deena firmly said. "Please?"

Her mom seemed caught off guard, as if she was not prepared for the moment. Deena watched as her mom squeezed her dad's hand. Deena wasn't sure if she was trying to wake him up, or if she was reassuring him of her own resolve.

Deena waited. Each passing second made

her increasingly nervous and worried. Jamal joined Deena in watching their mother.

"Yes," Mom said finally, meeting Deena's gaze. "It's not good. I promised your father we'd tell you in the morning, as a family, OK?"

"Mom, how can we wait that long? I can't wait."

"You can," Mom said.

Deena turned, left the room, and walked the long, dimly lit hallway. Her body filled with a new kind of adrenaline. Since her mother had returned to the waiting room an hour earlier, she'd been feeling worried and upset.

What was worse than bad news? Deena thought. *Knowing that bad news was coming!*

It was a special kind of torture, and Deena walked up and down the hallway in an effort to rid herself of it. Walking didn't help. Her legs felt bouncy, as if they contained springs.

During the ride home from the hospital, Deena said nothing. Her mother drove, while her father sat in the passenger seat, his right hand resting on the windowsill just as it always did. Deena sensed that the two of them had pre-arranged the circumstances in which they'd talk with their kids. Now they seemed determined to carry out the plan exactly, despite the obvious tension and worry that had been present for hours.

As they drove along next to the Schuylkill, Philadelphia's meandering river, Deena stared at each runner along the path, feeling that same restlessness in her muscles. She hadn't felt it before, but walking the hallways the previous night had filled her with a desire to stretch her legs and dash through the early-summer air.

Her family filed into the house quietly, each member of the family walking directly to the kitchen table at which they always ate dinner. Deena sat in her usual seat and watched as her father slid slowly into his chair at the end of the table. He took a deep breath and reached for his wife's hand.

Finally, Deena thought, *finally this black cloud overhead can at least start raining.*

"We have some bad news," Dad said, looking first at Deena and then at Jamal. He paused then, as if waiting for one of them to inquire about exactly what the bad news was. No one spoke.

"Last night, what I had was a mini-heart attack, nothing life-threatening in any way. By the time I got to the hospital, the pain in my chest was lessening." He touched his hand to where the pain had been and looked again at his wife. "But while I was back there, the doctors did a number of tests."

The house was quiet around them. The dishes from the previous night were piled haphazardly near the sink, which disturbed Deena as much as anything. She'd never seen this kitchen so dirty in the light of day. Her parents never went to sleep with dishes in the sink or on the counters. Oddly enough—considering their reluctance to talk to their kids these last twelve hours—her parents weren't procrastinators.

The neighbor's dog barked. Dad turned his head toward the noise, pausing once again in mid-thought.

"Dad," Deena said, more sharply than she would have liked. For her, this moment could not end soon enough. She needed to hear whatever words he held within him. She needed all of them to share this terrible thing.

"Hmm," Dad said, turning forward. He gave his wife's hand a quick squeeze and then said, "I have pancreatic cancer."

Like a bowling ball, the words landed with a thud in the middle of the table. All four of them, Deena included, seemed to be staring at the same point equidistant between them. No one's eyes ventured farther than precisely in the middle. Deena knew right then that the only thing keeping her from absorbing the full truth of that sentence was eye contact with either one of her parents. Until the moment she looked into her dad's eyes, this sentence about "pancreatic cancer" was connected to nothing. He could have said that the grass needed cutting or that he'd rather not have meatloaf for dinner again. But once she looked at her father, that would be the period at the end of the sentence, the final movement that made this news real and complete.

Deena moved her eyes slowly from the swirled grain of the wooden table. First she saw her father's hand. She noticed his gold wedding band. Then she saw the hair on his arms, and then the grey sleeve of his t-shirt. She moved her eyes higher, toward the stubble on his chin, which was noticeable because he hadn't yet shaved that morning. Finally, she raised her eyes to his and saw the pool of tears within them. She had never seen that before, and the sentence—"I have pancreatic cancer"—sent a wave of fear through her.

"Daddy," she whispered.

"I know, honey," he said quickly, reaching up and wiping away the tears that had not yet dropped. The four of them said nothing for a moment, each staring into their own space.

Deena didn't know how bad pancreatic cancer was, but she suspected the worst. Jamal, though, understood the word "cancer," but didn't know how "pancreatic" affected the diagnosis.

"You can beat this, Dad, right?" Jamal said, glancing between the three of them. For a second he locked eyes with Deena. He seemed confused by how quiet and scared she looked.

"Of course we're going to try," said Dad, offering a wisp of a smile to his son.

"Matt's mom had breast cancer a few years ago, you remember that?" Jamal continued. "Everyone was so sad and worried in the beginning, and now she's doing awesome. I saw her last week at the game, and it's like nothing ever happened."

"Well, yes." Dad searched for the right words. "This is a little different than that, though."

No one said anything for a few seconds. Deena watched her dad's eyes, wondering if more tears would form during the silence.

None did. Just when he seemed ready to say something more, something that might give Jamal a better understanding of exactly what they were fighting, the shrill ring of the house phone cut through the silence.

"We better get that," said Mom, who was at the phone before it rang a second time.

As the family left the table, Deena hurried back to her room. She noticed Jamal trailing her down the hallway. He seemed to want to come into her room and talk, but Deena closed the door quickly and walked to her computer. With trembling fingers, she opened up Google and typed "pancreatic cancer" into the search box. She tried three times before finally getting it right.

The search results quickly loaded onto the screen, and Deena closed her eyes against the words that appeared below the first result: *The worst kind of cancer.*

She took a deep breath and clicked the page anyway. She scanned the page that came up, and more terrible phrases appeared, each one taking more of her breath away:

Extremely low survival rate.

Unknown cure.

Fast progressing.

Not wanting to read any more, Deena closed the search page, fearing that if she allowed the results to stay on the screen, they would become more and more real. She knew her parents possessed the same information and wondered what questions they had asked their doctor.

How long have you known her?

Chapter 2

Deena was already awake when her alarm rang. Lying on her back, staring at the white ceiling, she'd been waiting for the alarm to finally announce itself. Hard to say how long she'd been awake. At least an hour, she thought, probably longer.

Relieved to be released from the prison of her bed and her thoughts, Deena silenced her high-pitched cell-phone alarm and sat on the bed's edge, planting her bare feet on the hardwood. She listened for the stirring of her parents in the room next to hers, but heard nothing but the whirl of the overhead fan. Then she padded down the hallway, careful not to wake the rest of her family. She knew her brother would be sound asleep. And she assumed her parents were still holed up in their bedroom.

It was only 6:30. Deena headed for the refrigerator, more out of habit than hunger. But as she reached the faded white fridge, she noticed a piece of loose-leaf paper held there with a magnet. A message, written in ink, was scribbled across its front.

Because she'd never seen anything attached to their refrigerator—there was no need for notes when everyone in the family text-messaged—the note seemed like something from another time: *Early morning treatment at hospital. Didn't want to wake you. Be back by 8 or so. We love you, Mom & Dad.*

Deena freed the note from behind the square magnet and carried it to the kitchen table. She slipped down into her chair and stared at the words as if they were written in a foreign language. Without warning, her chest tightened and tears came rolling into her eyes, as if she was filled with too much liquid and someone had poked a hole in her. She couldn't stop crying. She stared at the paper. Through her tears, the words appeared as if she was reading through a glass of water, all wavy lines and distorted.

Deena missed her parents more than she had in years.

She was alone in the kitchen. Their only

presence was this piece of paper. She crossed her arms on the wood and rested her head on them, her chest heaving. She stayed like that until, exhausted, she couldn't cry any more. And then she got ready for school.

There was only one class Deena cared about: English Literature. It was her final class of the school day, taught by her favorite teacher, Mr. Humphries, and consisting almost exclusively of her favorite things: good books.

She was, perhaps, the only student who felt this way, at least the only one who admitted it. The rest of her classmates cracked jokes about the reading they hadn't done, passed notes, and diminished the value of stories through which Deena had both laughed and cried.

Today's English Lit class promised to be special, but it also promised to be scary. As Deena walked down the hall toward the classroom, she could feel a wave of nerves wash over her.

For the previous month, they'd been reading *Great Expectations*, a book Mr. Humphries called "a masterpiece." He began the unit by showing the Hollywood film of the movie. Then each day that followed, he would read a scene in class and discuss its significance. Deena adored the story. She was even able to overcome her shyness enough to occasionally answer one of the questions that Mr. Humphries would ask.

But each time she spoke in class, she did so after battling extended moments of anxiety. She worried that what she said would be ridiculed, even though she knew her answers were correct. She'd seen her classmates ridicule everything, just for the sake of having fun.

The first time Deena had raised her hand, she'd done so tentatively, as if she was watching someone else. She expected all of her classmates to stare in amazement that the shy, quiet girl was speaking. But she overestimated their attention spans. Most of the other kids had their heads on their desks, and they didn't even notice that she'd spoken. After Deena answered that first question, she braced herself for her classmates' laughter, but the only sound she heard was a stifled yawn from somewhere in the back.

Then, to Deena's surprise, Mr. Humphries announced that on the last day of class, a number of students would be given "a part" in a class-long reading of his favorite scene from the book. And he cast Deena as the female lead. It was obvious that he trusted her and that she cared about the story. She would come prepared.

On that final day, Deena walked into the empty classroom, choosing to forego the five minutes of hallway time in favor of rereading the scene they would perform. She sat in the first row, as she always did, and buried her eyes in the pages. Her knee bounced up and down, the only external sign of her nervousness. As the minutes ticked past, she could hear the room filling. It had been years since her classmates last teased her without being provoked, but she still felt relieved when kids brushed past her and didn't say anything.

Deena struggled to focus on the words. Her concentration, once her great asset, had been shattered by the news of her father's cancer. It felt now as if her mind was consistently battling itself, with concern for her dad on one side and the demands of everyday life on the other.

On the final page of the scene Mr. Humphries had chosen, Deena caught herself, midway through the dialogue, picturing her father at his afternoon appointment. She moved her eyes to the page's top and tried again.

A minute later, Mr. Humphries rose from his desk, a book in his hand. He stepped to the front of the room. His slender figure and pointy features had always commanded less attention than most of Deena's other teachers, but his passion for the subject matter had won her over.

"All right, let's get started," he said. "Everyone take out your books."

Deena listened as everyone rummaged through their backpacks, grudgingly pulling tattered versions of *Great Expectations* from the depths of their bags. Deena closed her book and placed her palm on the book's cover. She tried to pin her heel to the floor to calm herself.

Mr. Humphries had written the number of the chapter they would be play-acting, along with everyone's role for the day, on the chalkboard. Her eyes landed on her own assignment, and she read her name, "Deena Jackson." Although seeing her name caused her knee to start bouncing frantically again, she liked how it looked. She liked her name on the board. She liked being chosen. She was somewhat surprised at the swell of excitement she felt over it, even though that excitement was battling nerves.

"Everyone turn to the beginning of Chapter 11." Deena was already there, staring at the printed words anxiously.

"Oh, come on!" came a boy's voice from the back of the room. "It's the last day. Do we have to do any more with this book? Can't we just hang out instead?"

Mr. Humphries looked over the top of his glasses. "No, young man, we cannot."

Different students in the class let out groans of protest, and everyone laughed. Deena let out a long breath as she realized the class shared none of her excitement. She felt dumb at being so eager to do something that everyone else thought would be boring. Her eyes burned, but she refused to produce tears. The burning behind her eyes was about so much more than the book in front of her, and her tears would attract attention she didn't want. She dropped her eyes from the book to her lap.

Mr. Humphries happened to glance down at her just then, and he offered her a barely perceptible shake of his head as encouragement. Deena averted her eyes.

The class was a disaster. The reading was a chore for everyone, including Deena. She suddenly felt drained of any energy, and wound up pretending to be bored because everyone else seemed to be. She injected little life into her character, reading her lines as if reading the back of a medicine bottle.

The bell finally rang, putting them all out

of their misery. Deena waited until the room cleared, a tactic she'd learned years ago in order to avoid walking between groups of friends of which she wasn't a part. She carefully placed her book in the small pocket in her backpack's front compartment and rose from her chair.

Mr. Humphries was sitting at his desk, watching her. "Deena," he said, lowering his glasses from his nose and letting his wrist dangle the wire frames in the space between them.

Deena clung to the straps of her backpack, now keenly aware that she had disappointed him.

He continued speaking once he had her full attention. "Don't let yourself fade into the background in school just because it feels easiest," he said.

And that, to Deena's surprise, was all he said.

Chapter 3

The summer was a month old, and Deena had already read a dozen books. She was nestled into her chair, about to begin the next novel.

"Honey!" her father called from the living room. "Can you come here for a second?"

Although it was phrased as a question, Deena knew it was more of a statement. She thought about pretending not to have heard, but knew that would only delay the inevitable for a minute—at most. She placed her book on the small table and rose from her chair. The falling rain was pelting the one window in the room, and Deena was glad for it. It allowed her to stay inside and read without guilt. On sunny days, she felt cooped up inside, but she still had little motivation to do anything outside.

Her long strides had her down the hallway in only four steps—it used to take her twelve when she was a little girl—and she poked her head around the corner at her father. "What is it, Dad?" she asked.

His eyes were closed. His head rested against the recliner. He hadn't been to work in over a week; the cancer treatments, and the cancer itself, had drained him of energy.

"Can you grab me a glass of water? My throat is dry."

"Sure," Deena said, "of course." She walked into the kitchen. Jamal was sitting at the table. His attention was focused on his hand-held game, and Deena noticed the ear buds in his ears. He hadn't heard anything. When he spotted her, he lifted his head and removed the earphones.

"What's up?" he asked, his eyes filled with worry.

Deena motioned for him to keep playing and said, "Dad just needs a glass of water." She filled a glass with tap water and placed it on the table next to her dad's chair. The TV was on in front of him. He was watching ESPN's *SportsCenter* on morning re-runs. She walked away, anxious to return to her book.

Just as she settled back into the overstuffed chair, her dad called again. "Baby girl?" she heard him say, weaker this time. "I need you."

A wave of annoyance washed over her. It was followed closely by guilt. The guilt pushed her back to her feet and sent her marching back down the hallway.

"Get the soup pot," her dad begged, "quickly."

Deena pulled open the drawers beneath the sink, believing her mother stored it there. She couldn't find it. She checked in the dishwasher and on the pot rack above the doorway. It wasn't there.

Jamal stood up from the table, but he remained motionless, seemingly unsure of how he could help. He watched his sister move from cabinet to cabinet, taking a step forward as if he might join her. But instead he turned quickly, walked back down the hallway, and closed himself in his room.

A sickening noise came from the living room, a retching followed by the sound of released liquid. Deena heard her dad groan, and then he began coughing and spitting. She kept looking for the soup pot, even though she knew it was no longer needed.

"Deena," her dad croaked.

She had been on tiptoes, searching the cabinets above the refrigerator. She slowly shut the cabinet doors and peeked around the corner into the living room. There was vomit on the floor, on the chair, and all over her dad. His eyes were lowered, but he raised them to hers.

"It came on so suddenly," he said, his voice soft and shaky.

"I know, Dad, it's OK."

"One minute I felt fine; the next I couldn't stop it."

"I know, Daddy, I know."

"I'm so sorry."

She walked toward him—two long steps. "No, don't be sorry, don't be." He kept looking into her eyes, seemingly unable to address the condition he was in.

"I'll fix it," Deena said, and darted back to the kitchen to collect everything she'd need. Returning with the paper towel roll, a plastic bag, and a container of disinfectant wipes, she knelt by her dad, whose head was again resting against the back of the recliner. His breaths were short and quick. She helped him raise his arms to the ceiling and peeled off his white t-shirt. She quickly used the shirt to gather up most of the spill and then bunched the shirt in on itself and stuffed it into the plastic bag.

"I'm sorry," she heard her father say, so softly it seemed not much more than a thought escaping his mind.

Deena put her hand on his forehead and became suddenly aware of how much weight he had lost in just the four weeks since treatments had begun. It was the twice-weekly chemo that had melted the fat from his once solid frame.

"It's not this bad," he said, opening his eyes. "It's just a bad day, baby, that's all it is, just one bad day."

"Tomorrow will be better," she said, hoping they both believed it.

Deena's breath caught in her chest. It felt as if there was a rock stuck in her throat, and the pain caught her off guard. Swallowing hard, she pulled out a fistful of disinfectant wipes and began cleaning his recliner. The plastic bag was soon filled with dirtied wipes, and the smell of lemon disinfectant helped offset the smell of the vomit.

If she had been home, Deena's mom would have been caring for her father, as Deena was now. But she was at the hospital.

She'd volunteered for extra shifts ever since her husband had been forced to stop working.

Deena pulled the sweatpants gently off her father, taking care not to twist his hips inadvertently. She added the pants to the plastic bag, tied a knot in the handles, and took the bag out to the garbage can. Closing the lid over the bag, she stood for a second, not caring that the rain was darkening her gray t-shirt.

She'd solved the situation; she'd made the problem disappear. She had a sense of relief. But it felt a little like surviving one wave while caught in a storm. There were surely many more to follow.

Deena bounded back into the house, looking now at a father exposed in only his boxer shorts. She had always thought of him as a powerhouse, but the man in front of her now was vulnerable and weak, shivering despite the heat of the summer. She felt her throat beginning to close, a choking feeling that pushed against her chest, but she swallowed. There was nothing she could do to protect him.

But instead of staring, instead of becoming trapped in that moment, she kept moving: to her parent's room for another t-shirt and a different pair of sweatpants.

Her father had fallen asleep. How was that possible? How could he not be caught in the same flood of emotions that she now felt? Gently, Deena nudged him awake and worked the clothes back onto him in the same way she'd once dressed her stuffed animals and dolls. Before she had finished, his head lolled to the side, again asleep. She kissed his forehead and walked slowly back to her room. Her book was still on the side table, just where she'd left it, and the brown overstuffed chair looked just as soft and inviting. But for whatever reason, Deena didn't want to sit in it. She didn't want to read anymore. She couldn't imagine getting lost in someone else's life when she was missing her own.

Deena paced the room for a few minutes. She couldn't sit. She couldn't read. She couldn't be inside this room for another minute. She sat on the edge of the bed and felt her body pulse with energy. Her knees were bouncing up and down, and Deena finally placed her hands on her knees and pinned her feet to the ground.

She loved books. She loved reading. But for too long she'd worn books like a mask: a defense against standing up and asking if she could sit in an open seat, if she could join a conversation.

Deena jumped off the bed and stood to her full height. Walking to her closet, she rummaged through it and found a pair of sneakers her dad had bought her last year. She'd never worn them. He had come home with them after work one day, still in their original box, and explained how he'd run a little bit in high school and he believed she could, too. She had accepted the gift tentatively, unsure if this meant her dad expected she begin running that very day, but he had mentioned the sneakers only once more.

"Have you tried out the sneakers I bought you?" he had asked one night while they were watching the Phillies game.

Deena had grunted a response, intending the noise to convey, "No."

"Well, they'll still fit." He kept his eyes on the TV. "I bought them a half size too big so you'd grow into them."

She now sat on the bed's edge and laced them, taking the time to double-knot the laces and checking a third time to make sure they wouldn't come undone. Then she walked quickly down the hallway and out the front door without even looking into the living room.

The afternoon was muggy because of the rain, but Deena burst into it without pausing.

She weaved through the parked cars and into the middle of the street, taking a right along the road that led to Fairmount Park.

The rain felt warm on her arms and face, and Deena lengthened her stride to gain speed. She had no idea how long she would run, or where she would go. But it felt good to be moving somewhere that her body—not her mind—was taking her. She didn't need to save energy for later because she'd just stop when she was tired. She was running as fast as she wanted to, right from the start.

The green trees of the park's edge came closer and closer until Deena arrived on the sidewalk that paralleled the park's edge. No longer in traffic's way, she focused on her feet hitting the pavement, and the thoughts spilling through her mind.

The sidewalk alongside the park was filled with uneven concrete, and Deena watched each of her steps, careful not to catch the rough edges between the squares. She found a rhythm, and after a few minutes she was able to lift her eyes from the ground and stare through the drizzling rain as the park curved around her. At first her thoughts were as freefalling as the rain: one thought after another came flooding through her mind. She forced herself to give each thought specific attention.

First, she focused on her father. The cancer was winning so quickly. Or was the treatment knocking him out? Was there any chance he could survive this? How had this happened to them—and why? What would she do without her dad? How would her family go on? There were things they hadn't yet discussed, and somehow Deena felt they might never discuss. And then it would be too late.

Deena remembered one Sunday when she was just a little girl. She and her dad had gone to church together, just the two of them. Jamal had been at a friend's house for a birthday sleepover, and her mom had begged off with a headache.

After church, they had driven home the long way, stopping by a Wawa for coffee and Danishes. Her dad had idled the long, silver Buick in front of the Wawa and put the sports radio station on low. The two of them did this sometimes: if Deena helped him return the empty bottles to the grocery store or if she joined him on an inspection of a job site over the weekend. It was his way of thanking her for her company, a reward she always anticipated, and Deena loved having her dad to herself.

On this Sunday morning, the car, filled with sunshine, was bright and warm. She had just finished her Danish, and she looked over at her dad, who was sipping his coffee with the morning paper spread across the steering wheel. "Do you believe in God?" she'd asked.

Instead of answering her immediately, Dad put his coffee back in the cup holder and carefully folded the paper back onto his lap.

"What's on your mind, baby girl?" he finally said, turning his full attention to her. He did this often, which is how she knew she'd said something important to him.

"Oh, I don't know, Daddy. I was just thinking at church about all of it. What they say about God."

"And what do you believe?"

"I don't know yet. I know I'm supposed to believe what they say," she'd said.

"No, honey, you're supposed to believe what's in your heart."

"Really?" She'd looked down at her feet, which were stuffed into an old pair of white church shoes that buckled over the top. "What's in your heart?"

"This is a very important conversation, perhaps the most important conversation a person can have."

Deena had pointed to his coffee and said, "I know, you even put down your coffee for it."

Her dad had laughed his deep, baritone laugh.

"That's true, isn't it? It's a put-down-the-coffee kind of conversation. Here's what I think, baby. I think believing in God can be a tricky thing because you never get to see Him. He's just an idea you have to put your faith in. For me, though, I like to cover all of my bases."

Deena thought of this day often. And she thought of it now as she ran past an overturned shopping cart at the park's edge. When she was little, this answer hadn't made much sense to her. But as she grew and began making her own decisions, she started to see the logic in her father's answer. And, perhaps more than anything, it began to represent the common sense on which her dad based his life. He would not blow you away with magical talent, but he would win you over with steady perseverance.

Remembering his answer—"I like to cover

all of my bases"—reassured her that her dad could handle anything in life. But her heart also ached because she knew this battle could not be won through anything he did. He couldn't show up early, stay late, and collect enough money to pay that month's hospital bill.

There were no rules. It was so unfair.

Deena picked up more speed, trying to outrun the wave of anger that had so suddenly built up in her. The world was so big. And she was so small inside of it. The rain came from far away and covered everyone for miles, more miles than she could ever run.

She kept running.

Off in the distance, Deena spotted a looming statue. She knew the park had statues at various entrance points. Each statue represented an important man from history, often from the American Revolution. She decided she'd touch the statue, see which specific famous man it honored, and then turn around for home. But as she came closer, she noticed a family piling into their station wagon. They were all watching her run, and she didn't want to stop or turn around with them watching. She didn't want them thinking she couldn't keep running this fast for even longer, or that she had just started running a few hundred yards before. So she kept her head level through the rain and sprinted right past the gigantic statue of a man on his horse.

It felt good, having those eyes on her. A rush of adrenaline had coursed through her, making her able to manage even more speed. She kept that pushed pace until the station wagon was well out of sight behind her. Alone on a turn inside the park, the final push of energy and adrenaline depleted from her body, Deena finally stopped and bent over her knees. She gasped for air, realizing instantly how exhausted she was.

How long had she been running? How far away from home was she? How would she get back?

The rainwater slid off Deena's nose. Her hair was plastered down, and her gray shirt was soaked through and pinned to her body. Still, she felt more alive than she had in weeks. She stood upright, hands on hips, and looked up into the falling rain. Her chest heaved with each breath. Only when she had rested for a few minutes did she begin walking back the way she'd come.

The rain had darkened the park's twisting roads, and the overhanging trees shimmered with freshly washed green leaves. A banged-up old truck thundered past, its passenger craning her neck at the sight of Deena—soaked through and through—slowly walking along the road.

Deena smiled. The rain continued falling.

When Deena finally got home, it was just after 5 o'clock, and her mother's car was parked by the curb. The rain had slowed to a drizzle when she'd been about halfway home. By the time she climbed the three steps of the stoop, the sun was peeking from behind the clouds, and she'd begun to sweat again.

Deena reached for the stainless steel doorknob and froze. She dropped her eyes down to her sneakers and allowed the fear to wash over her. What had she been thinking, just leaving like that? She twisted the knob and pushed herself through the door. "I'm so sorry," she panted as she stepped onto the plastic doormat.

The living room was empty. Her father's recliner was exactly where she'd left it, but he was no longer in it.

She didn't even remove her wet shoes. She flew down the hallway and into her parents' bedroom. "Dad," she cried out as she entered, fearing the worst.

She found her mom sitting in the small side chair next to their bed. She still wore her nurse's uniform. Her finger was raised to her lips.

"He's asleep," she said, pointing to the bed.

"Oh, Mom," Deena whispered, making her way to the other side of the room. "I'm so, so sorry."

"What do you mean?" Mom tilted her head.

Deena knelt next to the chair. "I left," she said.

"You left?"

"I had to leave. I just had to. I went running. I didn't tell anyone. I don't know what I was thinking."

"Everything is fine. Your father is just sleeping."

Deena exhaled. "I don't know what I was thinking," she said again.

"Honey," her mom whispered, "it's not your job to take care of him."

"Yes, it is." She looked up into her mom's eyes.

"No, it's not."

"We had an awful day today. He got really sick this afternoon. Out of nowhere. There was nothing I could do to stop it."

Mom was softly nodding her head.

"I was cleaning it all up, and he was so tired and skinny. Mom, do you know how skinny he is now? It seems like it happened all of a sudden. I had to take off his t-shirt, and there's so much of him gone. It scared me. I went back to my room to read, and it was like I couldn't be inside one more minute."

Her mom said nothing. She placed her soft, worn hand on Deena's cheek and continued nodding.

"I ran until I couldn't run anymore. It took me over an hour to walk home. And the weirdest thing was that I wasn't even worried about leaving Dad until I got home. Right then it hit me that I'd just left him here, just left him sleeping without anyone else in the house."

Deena stopped talking and let her head drop. She could feel her mom's attention turn toward the doorway, and so Deena lifted her eyes as well. Jamal, who somehow seemed to have gotten smaller, was standing tentatively on the threshold. His right hand was gripping the doorframe as if he wasn't so sure of himself, and his left hand was dangling by his side.

Mom motioned for him to come over to them. Jamal walked over and crawled under her arm the way he used to, making himself small and soft.

"Babies," Mom said after a long pause. She put her other hand on Deena's other cheek, cupping her daughter's face. "It's just going to keep getting worse. Sometimes it'll feel slow, like this is all we've ever known. Other times it will fly past, like we're losing him more quickly than we can handle. We'll all need to run away—just like you did today, baby girl—but the only important thing is that we eventually come back home."

Deena let her tears roll over her mother's hands. The tears fell onto her t-shirt, but rain and sweat had already soaked it through. Jamal's shoulder was touching Deena's, and she could feel the rise and fall of his chest, even though she could not hear him crying.

Deena watched as he lifted his head and asked, "Why is this happening to Dad?" It seemed as if he genuinely wanted an answer.

Mom shook her head and said, "There is no 'why,' Jamal, and you can't spend your time trying to find one. Instead, make sure Dad knows how much you love him."

Deena looked into her mom's eyes and said the one thing she couldn't bring herself to say—until now. "I don't want him to die, Mommy,"

Deena sobbed, not caring that she'd lost control. "I don't want him to die."

That night the four of them ate dinner at the kitchen table just as they always used to do. Jamal sat across from Deena, and their dad sat at the head of the table.

Dad picked at the food on his plate. His appetite had vanished, and watching him eat was like looking at a baby bird after years of seeing a ravenous lion. He used his fork to spear the smallest carrot on his plate. No matter how little he actually consumed, he kept his fork going as if that would trick everyone into thinking he was eating a lot.

"Mom tells me you went running today," he said to Deena.

She nodded. It had felt so good. Even now, hours later, her body was still radiating energy, as if she'd lit herself from the inside. But Deena only nodded, not wanting her dad to know how alive she'd felt. Not wanting him to know that for a good chunk of the run, her mind had been cleared of everything happening to him, and she had cared only about the sound of her sneakers on the pavement and her heart thudding in her chest.

"I always knew you'd be a runner," he said. "Those long legs of yours were made for running."

"Daddy, I'm not a runner. I just happened to go running . . . today."

"Where did you run?"

"Oh, I don't know. I just kept running until I had to stop."

"Baby girl." He lowered his fork now, and Deena couldn't help noticing how heavy the silverware looked in his hand. "You know I did track and field in high school. Held the school record for the discus throw for three seasons. Now tell me about this run of yours."

She glanced from her dad to her mom and then across the table to Jamal, who was having trouble communicating with the same energy he used to have. It was taking so much restraint not to explode with every detail of the run. She wanted to tell them about how her legs moved perfectly together, how she'd found just that last bit of energy when the family had been watching. Would it be OK to talk about these things?

"I ran on the outside of the park until I saw that monument," she finally said. "I ran a little bit past that, then stopped and walked home."

"Which monument?" he asked.

"The one by the crossing, with the man on the horse."

"Near the Kelly Drive opening?" His voice rose.

"Yes, that's the one," she said.

Dad tilted his head sideways, as he always did when he was calculating something, like whether or not they could afford new basketball sneakers for Jamal, or if they should renew their membership to the YMCA. When Deena stayed up too late and shuffled to the kitchen for a glass of water, she often saw her parents huddled over the kitchen table, and her dad would have his head tilted this way.

"Five miles!" he exclaimed. The quick exhale seemed to catch him off guard, and he began coughing as if something was stuck in his throat. Mom popped from her chair and knelt next to him, rubbing his back. He waved her away, eventually swallowing.

"It's just over five miles to that crossing." His eyes were shining.

Deena had no idea how far she'd run. "Wow," she said. "I've never run more than a mile before."

"And you just walked back?" he asked.

"Yes, I couldn't run any farther."

"I imagine you couldn't," he said, still looking as if he was calculating something.

A silence dropped over the table. Deena scrambled for something to say, any bit of conversation that would continue the diversion and move the dinner closer to its conclusion.

"How is basketball camp?" she asked her brother.

"It's fine," he said, not even looking up from his plate.

"That's it? Just fine?"

He shrugged his shoulders. "Yeah, I don't know. Whatever. It's fine."

"Last summer, you'd have told us every story from camp and how your behind-the-back dribble was coming along," Mom chimed in.

Jamal raised his eyes to Deena's. The two of them looked at each other for a long moment, and Deena could feel everything he wasn't saying: *That was last summer; everything is different; I don't know what to say anymore.*

"It's going well," Jamal said at last. "Two days left. My team is in first place."

"Well, that's good," their mom offered.

"Yup," he said.

Deena looked down at her plate. It was

divided into three areas: broiled chicken, carrots, and mashed potatoes. She looked at the colors and the food and then rested her fork across the plate. She felt like running again, but knew she couldn't. For one, it was too late. For another, everyone here needed her, and she couldn't just disappear again.

The silence that Deena had fought draped across the table for one second, then another. The seconds piled on top of each other, so many of them that she no longer felt bothered by the quiet.

"It's over five miles!" her dad said, startling all of them.

No one responded.

"Yeah, it has to be. Because I take that route to work when Kelly Drive is backed up. I use the back roads by the park. It's more than five miles. It has to be. I think it's closer to six!"

Chapter 4

It was early afternoon when Deena put down her latest book—this one about the art of running—and went to see her dad. At the start of the summer, Deena had walked to the library and checked out a stack of books about running and training. She was halfway through the pile and now felt like a running expert: she knew how to train, how to race, how to eat, how to stretch, how to stay mentally strong. The library had an entire shelf of books about running.

Her dad was dozing in his chair, watching the Phillies afternoon game against the Washington Nationals. He drifted in and out of sleep while Deena, on the couch next to him, watched the fourth inning. A sliver of afternoon sunlight slipped in through the drawn curtains—too much light worsened his headache—and she propped her feet on the arm of his chair.

Dad slowly pulled himself awake and sat taller in the recliner. The effort seemed to steal his breath. He took one of her socked feet in his hands and began massaging the arch. "What's on tap for today?" he asked.

"Long run," she said, "over an hour."

"How do you feel?"

"Good, ready for it."

"How's the Achilles?" He moved his fingers to the back tendon above her heel and pressed into the flesh as deeply as he could.

"OK, I think. The ice has really helped, and taking the weekend off was probably a good idea."

As the summer had progressed, they'd developed a routine—just the two of them. She'd come to enjoy it as much as her books. Now, the two of them talked about her running.

When Deena was ready to hit the pavement, she came out to the living room and discussed the workout for the day with her dad. He didn't know much about running workouts, but he'd called in a favor and gotten a summer running plan from one of the area coaches. The two of them had followed it exactly.

Usually, a baseball game, or a replay of a game, was on the TV when she made her way out to the living room. If it wasn't the Phillies game on the local channel, it was a national game on ESPN. After resting with him for an inning or two, she'd lift her feet to the side of his chair, and he'd massage her arches and Achilles tendons.

Deena used this time as a barometer of her dad's strength and health. Some days, his hands really dug into her sore muscles, while other days his touch was so weak it wasn't more than a caress. She didn't need his work as a massage therapist, but she loved how happy her running made him.

"You think you're OK to run today?" he asked.

"Definitely. The weekend was more than enough time. Even yesterday, I wanted to get back out there."

He mumbled his approval. Deena could see that his strength was quickly leaving him. She pulled her feet off of his chair and planted them on the ground. "Time to go," she said.

"Remember on these long runs, it's all about your breathing. You want to be pushing yourself past the threshold, but holding your breathing as steady as possible." Dad had spoken with the area coach twice already. He'd asked him questions about each day's plan and how to get the most out of this summer.

"Yup, you got it." Deena walked toward the door and bent down to lace up her sneakers.

The summer's plan had helped, but Deena didn't have the heart to tell her dad that she already, instinctively, knew the goal for each day's run. She could feel the moments when her body was being taken to another level. She saw these as approaching waves, and she knew how to rise up and glide over them. The more she ran, the more she knew how good she was at running. But each time her dad offered one of these nuggets of wisdom, she embraced it as if it was the key to that day's run.

"See you in an hour, baby," he said, his eyes already closing.

"Bye, Daddy." She pushed herself through the front door and out into the day's heat and humidity.

Deena squinted against the glare and then dangled her head by her knees. She pulled herself tight, loosening her hamstrings. She folded herself together and took a number of deep breaths as her muscles began to awaken. Slowly pulling herself up, she walked over to her dad's truck and alternately stretched her calf muscles. She was in control; she knew her muscles intimately. Without additional procrastination, she set out from the driveway toward the park.

These long runs were Deena's favorites because they allowed her time to think without the burden of oxygen deprivation. At certain points during other runs—especially when she did intervals—her pulse was so fast she could think of nothing else but sucking in the next breath and hoping her aching muscles received just a little bit of oxygen. But on these hour-long runs, she could keep her breathing steady and her mind free to solve whatever problems needed solving. Running was like therapy. Slowly, even the most tangled knots loosened with each passing mile.

Deena settled into a strong, solid pace she could hold for an entire hour. She quickly did the math in her mind and figured she'd finish a little over eight miles during the hour. She could have easily cranked out a little more, but that wasn't the purpose of this run. Deena had to constantly remind herself of this. Often, her pace would creep faster without her actively trying, and she'd have to slow herself.

As she veered onto the shaded blacktop of the park, she allowed herself to attack the problem that had recently kept her awake at night. Could she go to college? Where might she go to college? Could her parents afford it? She had always assumed she'd be able to go, but everything had changed with her dad's cancer. They were making less money. Not only was her dad no longer working overtime; now her dad couldn't work at all.

Last summer, her parents had talked about this summer as being the time when they would go look at schools. But that hadn't happened. No one had mentioned anything about it. Deena was hesitant to raise the topic because it included future plans, and she'd noticed that recently her family had stopped discussing the future. It was as if talking about a year from now was like pushing her father into a black hole.

But in just under a year, Deena would graduate from high school. In a year, she could be packing up her things and preparing to move into her freshman dorm. More than anything, she wanted this opportunity to reinvent herself. She could go from being the dorky, friendless girl at Ben Franklin High into the confident, athletic woman she felt she was becoming.

As the park's trees flew past her, Deena noticed how fast she was running—much faster than the pace she'd intended. She slowed and began attacking the problem in another way.

Maybe she should just talk to her mom? Deena was convinced her parents' silence on the matter wasn't a calculated oversight, but rather the product of the messiness and confusion of the last three months. If she could just sit down with her mom, everything would be all right.

The miles ticked past, and Deena knew exactly how far she'd run: closing in on five miles. She was reaching the park's far edge. Usually this was where she'd take a left and begin circling back home. But today she ran past the bronze statue guarding the park's entrance. She continued onto the bike path that bordered the Schuylkill and ran along Kelly Drive.

The bike path, always crowded on the weekends, was nearly empty. Every few minutes, Deena would pass another runner. She noticed how fatigued and weary each looked. The midday heat was intense.

She knew exactly where she was headed. She just wasn't sure what she'd do when she arrived.

Deena had spent very little of the summer running through dense, city streets. But now she found herself watching the pavement for potholes and dips. She cut diagonally through the Fairmount neighborhood and crisscrossed toward her destination, careful to time the lights and look both ways.

She knew she'd have too long a run home, but that didn't matter now. She took a sharp left on Broad Street and, within seconds, found herself standing in front of her destination: Ben Franklin High's track. It was here the school held track meets and football games, about a half mile north of the school.

Deena looked at the sign bearing her school's name. Everything felt different this afternoon because, for the very first time, she wasn't there to trudge inside the halls and dutifully answer questions no one else could answer.

She was there to run.

Deena jogged alongside the fence until she saw the turnstile. There was a thick lock preventing entrance, but the turnstile was just waist-high. Deena surprised herself as she placed her palms on the metal and gracefully lifted herself inside.

How nice it felt, doing what she wanted.

Once inside, she looked out across the track. It was old, but appeared nicely kept; the grass looked freshly cut, and the track itself was free of holes and divots.

Deena walked back along the last straight-away, stretching her arms and allowing her breathing to become regular. Although she hadn't been running incredibly fast, she had covered a little over six miles. She took a few minutes to stretch her muscles. By the time she began walking back toward the starting line, her heart rate was approaching normal.

She glanced down at her watch—her father's watch, which he had lent to her when she'd begun running—and cleared the previous time, holding down the button until a string of zeroes showed on the watch's face. She toed the starting line. Her right hand was fingering the watch's start button.

She was ready. She took one more deep breath, filling her lungs until they hurt, and then took off in the same instant she started the watch.

She had no plan. She did not know if she would run one lap, or two, or ten. For two months, she had run only inside her own head, knowing when she was pushing herself based on her breathing, but not on mile markers and running time.

Today would be different. She was anxious to know what the watch would tell her.

The track baked in the afternoon sun. Deena kept her eyes forward, always looking at the next 100-yard marker in front of her. First it was the one off the first turn, then the faraway mark at the end of the back straightaway. She fought the urge to glance at her watch with each passing 100 yards. She kept repeating the advice her dad had given her a few weeks ago before a short sprint workout: Keep your head on the target and never look behind you.

Never look behind you. Never turn around to see who might be gaining ground. Always look forward. Always look at the goal in the distance.

Deena crossed the starting line, finishing the first lap, but she refused to look at the time. She knew she was running fast, about as fast a pace as she could hold over the distance of a mile.

She would run a timed mile, she decided. And with the distance decided, she kicked her stride a little longer, collected just a little bit more speed, telling herself this was the second of four laps. She was nearly halfway.

Eyes up. Each step pushing you closer. Don't think about anything but the finish line. She'd learned so much from the books she'd read.

Deena crossed the starting line for the second time, once again ignoring the watch. The third lap, she told herself, would be the last difficult one. The fourth lap would be the final lap, each step the last of the race, each moment the last chance to run faster. So the third lap would be the gut lap. She watched as the faraway curve approached. Then she put it behind her and refocused her eyes on the finish line.

As she raced across the starting line for the third time, she pushed just a little faster. This was it. Her breathing was short and quick. Her heartbeat was throbbing in her collarbone, something she noticed happened when she pushed herself past the typical threshold. The faraway curve disappeared under her sneakers, and she opened up into an all-out sprint. Peeling around the last curve, she faced the final straightaway and gobbled up the track.

Deena was running as fast as she'd ever run. Each step launched her toward the finish line, and she caught air when her right foot struck the track and when her left pushed off, extended, behind her. For that split second, it was as if she was flying.

She hit the stop button on her watch as she crossed the finish line. But she still didn't look at the result. About 20 yards past the line, she finally pulled to a stop. She tilted back her head, gasping for breath as if she were trying to drink rainwater. Her hands gripped her hips. Her chest heaved up and down, desperate to deliver oxygen to all the parts of her body.

She continued walking, out past the first curve and then into the back straightaway. Her heart rate began to calm, and she could once again walk normally, arms at her sides instead of on her hips or locked behind her head. Her time was like an anticipated secret on her wrist. She just kept breathing and tried not to think what the time might be.

How fast *had* she run? She really had no idea because she had nothing previous to compare it to. She knew she could often run 7:30-minute miles for her long runs, which meant that on some of the shorter ones, she was going much faster.

But for one mile?

Deena crossed the finish line again, completing her cool-down walk, and pulled off into the grass. Collapsing onto her back, she stared into the blue sky and white clouds, her eyes half open against the sun. It was finally time to look. She closed her eyes and lifted her left wrist about six inches in front of her face. She'd be happy with anything under six minutes, she told herself—just let it be under six minutes.

Deena opened her eyes, and there, etched in abbreviated dark lines on the watch's face, was her time: 5:07. She closed her eyes, opened them again. 5:07. She checked to ensure that the number wasn't the actual time of day, although she knew it was only early afternoon.

She stared at the number for a few seconds and then dropped her wrist to the grass and allowed a huge grin to spread across her face. She stared into the sky, the heat of the day feeling nice against her sweaty skin. Her heart was strong and clean in her chest. Her legs were strong and flexible underneath her. For the first time in her life, she felt completely alive.

Peeling herself off the infield grass, Deena stood. Then she caught movement out of the corner of her eye, and turned to look at the track's entrance. Her heart dropped. She looked around for another exit, but there wasn't one. She was trapped.

Carly and Monique jogged onto the track. They were laughing and talking to each other, not paying attention to anything else. When they slowed to a walk, Carly noticed Deena standing on the infield grass. Carly froze and tapped Monique, pointing at Deena as if she was an intruder in their home.

Deena ducked her head and tried to walk quickly past.

"Hey," she heard one of them call out. Deena ignored them, making it a few feet from the track entrance before she heard them again.

"Hey! Stop!"

Deena slowed and turned toward the girls. Her heartbeat felt faster than when she'd been running. She said nothing, assuming that turning towards them was her way of acknowledging their presence.

"What are you doing here?" Monique asked. She squinted her eyes, as if looking more closely would reveal an answer.

"I came to run."

"*You* run?" Carly didn't seem angry as much as confused.

"What's your name again?" Monique asked, even though Deena had been in the same classes with her for years. Deena surprised herself by wanting to say something rude in response, but instead fell back into her old, submissive behavior.

"Deena," she said. "Deena Jackson."

Monique nodded. "Oh, yeah, that's right."

The two girls looked at her for another second and then seemed to lose interest. "Bye, bye," Monique said, which sounded more like a dismissal than a farewell.

Deena turned, feeling her face flush. She exited the turnstile and turned right onto the cement of a city block. She began the long jog home, her anger lessening with each step. By the time she was nearing home, she had convinced herself that the interaction had been harmless. She'd simply misunderstood Carly and Monique's tone.

Maybe, Deena told herself, *maybe Monique really didn't remember my name.* Regardless, the moment had tainted her excitement about her mile time, and she pushed herself through her front door, feeling much more tired than she should have.

Her father was just where she'd left him— still sleeping. "Daddy," she said, putting a hand on his shoulder.

He slowly opened his eyes. "How long was I gone?" she asked.

"I don't know, baby. I fell back asleep." He pulled himself up in the chair to glance at the broadcast of the baseball game. "It's the eighth now, so you've been gone a while."

"Feeling OK?" she asked.

"I'm OK," he said with a sly grin. "I have a surprise for you." He nudged his head in the direction of the hallway bedrooms.

"A surprise?" She couldn't imagine what it could be, or how he might have managed any sort of surprise. He could barely brush his teeth without help.

"In your room," he added.

Deena squeezed his shoulder and walked toward her bedroom. The last time her dad had surprised her was years ago, when she was in first grade. It was the day after her birthday. She'd desperately wanted a puppy, but her parents had said a puppy was too much responsibility. Instead, she'd gotten a puzzle that she never actually opened. When she came home from school the day after her birthday, her dad's truck was in the driveway, surprising her, because he was never home in the afternoon. She had raced inside, and there sat her dad, on the floor in the middle of the living room, entertaining a black Labrador puppy.

Deena had named the dog Fern in honor of the book she was reading then. Fern had lived for eight years, and he often went to work with her dad. Fern had loved her dad best; even Deena knew that.

Fern died when Deena was a freshman in high school. Her dad had explained that sometimes big dogs didn't live as long, especially Labradors. He also said that Fern's heart had been too big for him. Deena had found this comforting, and now whenever she thought of Fern, she pictured him running through a wide open meadow, a version of dog heaven.

What might this surprise be? Deena was not expecting much, considering how limited her dad's mobility had become.

She opened her bedroom door and stepped inside. There it was, hanging on the wall above her bed: a framed poster of a beautiful woman in midstride. The image was printed in black and white and showed the young woman in the final steps of what appeared to be an excruciating race. Her muscles were contracted, and her face was steeled with grit and determination.

Underneath the image were the printed words, "Wilma Rudolph, the world's fastest woman, 1940–1994."

Deena couldn't even remember what used to hang in the space above her bed. The poster mesmerized her. It was perfect. She walked back to the living room, a cry caught in her throat.

"Thank you," she said to her dad. "Who is she?"

"She was a pioneer," he said, and he opened his arms so she could nestle inside for a hug. "She was so fast that if you blinked, you missed her." And then he added, "She was a star, baby girl, and so are you."

Deena didn't allow herself to cry.

Chapter 5

It was the dog days of August, with the city melting beneath heat and humidity. The start of Deena's senior year was two weeks away. And this morning was the first day of cross-country tryouts.

Deena had been awake since 6 a.m. First she showered, a long shower that would loosen her muscles. Then she set about making herself a breakfast of egg whites and turkey bacon.

The tryouts were open to everyone, but Deena felt as if she was invading them. Ben Franklin was not considered a strong cross-country school because the fall season carried only one long distance race: 5K, equivalent to 3.125 miles. Most of the girls ran cross-country as a warm-up for the winter indoor track and field season, which was itself only a warm-up for the more prestigious outdoor track and field season.

These were girls Deena knew by name only. They had been running together for so many consecutive seasons that they were more like sisters than classmates or teammates. Ben Franklin might have been average at cross-country, but it dominated at track and field.

Deena sat at her kitchen table, a plate of egg whites, turkey bacon, and wheat toast in front of her. She said a small prayer over the meal—something her dad would have said if he could still sit at the head of their table—and then set about eating it despite the nerves swimming in her stomach.

It wasn't the running that unnerved her. It was meeting the new group. The other girls would know their place, but Deena would tiptoe around, unsure, like a guest in someone's home. Running had been something she did alone. Today that would change; it would become something she did with others.

Finishing her breakfast, Deena climbed into the passenger's side of her mom's car. She gripped her water bottle between her two hands as if it was a bouquet of flowers and stared down at her double-knotted sneakers.

"You're nervous," her mom observed, turning over the engine.

Deena nodded, swallowing hard.

Her mom navigated in reverse out of their driveway and slowly pulled into the street. Deena felt a little bit like throwing up. She was glad she knew exactly how far it was to Ben Franklin High: 5.2 miles. She'd run it a few times toward the end of the summer. In the car, she had about 20 minutes with stoplights and traffic. She hoped it took 30 minutes. Her legs tingled with nerves and excitement. Despite the day's impending heat, she shivered, and goose bumps appeared on her arms.

"But you've been running so much," her mom said, spinning the wheel for a left turn.

Her mom had been too preoccupied to know what she'd been doing this summer. Mom had taken extra shifts at the hospital to make up the difference in salary. And when she was home, she was glued to the phone, making calls to various doctors and research centers in the hopes of finding a new cancer treatment. In her spare time, she was either tending to her husband or—and Deena knew she didn't get enough of this—sleeping.

On two occasions, Deena had carefully

entered her parents' room, hoping to talk about college with her mom. Both times, her mom had been asleep in her jeans: curled in a ball on top of the covers, as if at any moment she might be called to duty.

Needless to say, Deena had spoken very little with her mom about her running. That territory had been her dad's alone, which was fine. But it made Deena a little sad that her mom was missing the one thing at which she was so good.

And it was just two weeks from the start of her senior year, but Deena still hadn't spoken with either of them about college. She kept telling herself it was only a matter of time. But early applications were due in October.

"Honey," her mom spoke again. "You're going to be great."

"You have no idea what it's going to be like, Mom," Deena said.

Her mother changed her grip on the wheel and stared straight ahead as if Deena hadn't said anything. She navigated the car through the familiar streets on the way to Ben Franklin. Neither said anything else, although Deena chastised herself for adding something else to her mom's plate: an ungrateful, moody daughter. She kept telling herself to apologize, even opening her mouth a few times with the expectation she would do just that. But each time, she closed her mouth and kept quiet.

Her mom took the final turn onto Broad Street and crept to a stop directly in front of the high school. Nobody was there yet.

"Here you go, honey," her mom said. "I love you."

"I love you, too," Deena said as she climbed out of the car. She shut the door behind her and watched as her mom gave her a brief wave and drove away.

Deena lowered her head and walked to the school's front steps. She placed her water bottle, now perspiring and slippery, on the first concrete step and sat down next to it. She looked at her watch: 9:32. The first practice was to begin with a 10 o'clock meeting by these doors, after which they would jog to the track for their first run.

Chin in hands, Deena watched as people walked past. Most people appeared to be on their way to work. The heart of Philly, City Hall, was just a few blocks south on Broad Street. She thought about standing and stretching, keeping herself loose, but she felt deflated after the car ride with her mom. She'd just wait and see.

After about ten minutes, a beat-up Chevy pulled up to the front of the school, and out climbed three girls. Deena immediately recognized them as members of the track and field team: Carly, Sasha, and Monique. Deena lifted her head from her hands, anxious as to what these girls might do.

Carly, long and agile, was widely known as the school's best runner. Sasha and Monique were both shorter, stockier, but fast nonetheless. They were better on the sprints. They trailed after Carly, chattering. Carly eyed Deena sitting on the step and then glanced at the water bottle by her feet. It was clear why Deena was here.

Carly shifted her eyes away and led her group to the far side of the steps, well away from where Deena was sitting. Deena, who'd been hopeful that the girls would come sit with her, allowed herself to slump back onto the step. She considered standing and walking over to where they sat, but something told her she shouldn't. These girls knew who she was. Deena had been in biology last year with Carly. She'd taken Spanish with Sasha and English with Monique. There was no sense pretending they hadn't chosen to sit away from her.

Deena felt like walking away. She'd spent the summer building a new world for herself, but here she was living the same life she'd always lived. Running was better when she could stay inside her own mind. Nothing she did would ever be good enough for people like Carly or her classmates at Ben Franklin. She was invisible and always would be.

Unsure of what she should do next, Deena stood up from the step. What would she tell her dad? He was asleep at home right now, but when he awoke, he would want to hear all about how she had done. She thought of the poster of Wilma Rudolph now hanging above her bed. Just last night she had finished reading a biography of Rudolph. She learned that Rudolph had been born prematurely and had spent most of her life fighting racism and oppression.

Deena sat back down on the step.

Soon, the steps began filling with girls. Deena recognized almost everyone from either classes or the high school's hallways. No one came to sit next to her. A few cast surprised glances her way, as if she were most definitely in the wrong place. Those looks said, "*What are* you *doing here?*"

As 10 a.m. approached, Deena kept her eyes down. If she could just hold still until then, she'd have set the ball in motion. It would be that much more difficult to back out.

"Hey everyone!" called a familiar voice. Deena lifted her head to find who was speaking, but she couldn't immediately locate the voice. She stood up.

"Welcome, everyone, to the first day of cross-country tryouts," the man continued.

Deena finally spotted the speaker. It was Mr. Humphries, her English Lit teacher. Standing next to him was Coach Walker, a stout woman that Deena recognized as the school's cross-country and track coach. She placed herself just a step behind Mr. Humphries, as if wanting to make a statement by putting herself in his shadow.

Just as Deena felt out of place, Mr. Humphries seemed out of place, also. All of the surrounding girls started whispering among themselves. Deena had never seen him in anything but khakis and a button-down, but here he was in running shorts and a t-shirt.

Mr. Humphries cleared his throat. "I know this is a surprise for most of you, but we've had a last-minute substitution," he said. "Coach Walker found out last week that she's expecting, and she asked if I would take over for her this cross-country season."

He allowed that information to land on his audience. Most of the older girls, Deena noticed, turned to one another. Each of them had concerned expressions.

Coach Walker stepped forward. "Girls, I know this was unexpected," she began, instinctively touching her stomach. "And I wish the timing was different, but these things can't be planned." She went on to explain what would happen that season, how much she would be available, and the role that Mr. Humphries would play.

When Coach Walker finished speaking, a few seconds of silence followed. Finally, Carly spoke up. "So you won't be coaching us at all?" she asked.

"I'm afraid not," Coach Walker said, tilting her head in apology.

Mr. Humphries cleared his throat again and said, "I'll be the head coach. I spoke with Coach Walker last night, and she said she would be stopping by as often as she could, but that she had no way of knowing when that would be."

Mr. Humphries looked at the contingent of girls. There were about 35 girls present, which meant that some wouldn't make any of the teams: freshman, junior varsity, or varsity. As he scanned the faces in front of him, his eyes met Deena's. For a second, the two just stared at each other as if they'd run into one another on the street corner of a foreign country: *How is it possible we're both in this place?*

Mr. Humphries tilted his head. A smile crossed his lips. He held Deena's eyes for a moment before turning his attention elsewhere. The group in front of him was still buzzing with the news about Coach Walker.

"If everyone could have a seat on the steps," he called, shepherding the few standing girls toward the stairs. When everyone was seated, and when the buzz had calmed to a manageable level, Mr. Humphries laid out the guidelines of the fall cross-country season.

"We'll be keeping ten runners for varsity," he began. Everyone on the steps began glancing around at one another, as if guessing who those ten runners might be. Deena lowered her eyes.

Even with the change of coaching staff, Mr. Humphries explained, there was expected to be no drop-off in effort or expectations.

Deena sat in the far back corner, shaded by the building's shadow. As Mr. Humphries spoke, she began to relax. She wasn't the only unexpected newbie showing up today. She was ready for this, and she was used to excelling on her own, although usually she did so inside a classroom.

As his opening speech came to a close, Mr. Humphries asked for those trying out for varsity to gather together to his right. Deena stood, looking around at the other girls standing. There were twelve girls, all of them looking around and assessing the competition. Deena made her way to the gathering point. She knew all of the other girls, and she knew she was the only one trying out for her first season of running. But since she was a senior, varsity was the only team she was allowed to try out for.

Deena stood on the outskirts of the group as Mr. Humphries gathered the junior varsity and freshman hopefuls. "OK," he continued. "Warm-up jog to the track. Varsity, you lead the way, but stay on the sidewalks and be safe."

As they began the slow jog up Broad Street,

Deena hung toward the back. She could have easily darted to the front. The pace was slow, but she didn't want to draw attention to herself. Mr. Humphries started at the front and then slowly drifted through the pack until he was next to her.

"Fancy meeting you here," he said.

"I know," she replied. "I had no idea you coached cross-country."

"Until about a week ago, I didn't. I had no idea you ran cross-country."

"Until a few months ago, I didn't."

"Then we have something else in common," he said, winking at her before drifting backward toward the junior varsity group.

Deena had trouble keeping such a slow pace. She would find herself drifting forward. She would rein in her speed and fall back to her spot. Luckily, the jog wasn't long, and within a few minutes the throng was weaving through the gate and settling onto the infield grass of Ben Franklin's track.

Carly, who was captain of last year's team, immediately began leading the group through a series of stretches. Mr. Humphries said nothing. He walked around, clipboard in hand, asking each girl to spell her name.

Deena concentrated on her stretching. She pinned her forehead to her knees and breathed deeply.

"Here's the game plan," Mr. Humphries said as soon as Carly finished the final stretch. "Each group will run a timed mile. While one group is going, the others will jog slowly in the outside lanes to stay warm. The times will be recorded, so give it your best." He then added, "First up is the freshman group."

Deena walked to the general area where Carly and the other varsity girls were standing, making sure to separate herself from the freshman group and from the junior varsity. While the freshman group crowded around the starting line, the other groups began jogging on the outside lanes. Deena stayed a few feet behind the top group and settled into her jog.

A few feet ahead, the varsity girls were whispering back and forth, occasionally shooting glances back at her. Deena cast her eyes down and watched her feet rhythmically hit the track. Then she heard Carly say, "I'll do it," and in the next instant Carly was at Deena's left shoulder.

"We want to know what you're doing here," Carly said without hesitation.

"Just trying out for the team," Deena said,

in a voice so soft Carly had to lean forward to hear her words.

"But why? You've never tried out before."

"I just started running over the summer."

"We already have our starting varsity runners."

"Oh," Deena said.

"We don't need anyone coming in here ruining it."

"That's not what I'm trying to do."

"Just be careful," Carly said, and then took a few long strides to relay the conversation to her friends.

Deena was suddenly eager for the varsity's timed mile.

"I'll be calling out the running times for each lap," said Mr. Humphries, holding the stopwatch aloft.

Deena was in the third layer of girls, all of whom were crowding for position around the starting line. She could see Carly and her friends relaxing at the front. All five toed the starting line. Deena had decided she wouldn't force her way to the front. She didn't think she'd be fighting for each second, anyway. She lingered near the back, a few yards off the starting line, and waited for Mr. Humphries to drop his hand. She felt excited, as if she was about to display superhuman power, shocking everyone who thought she was just the class bookworm.

She smiled to herself just before Mr. Humphries dropped his hand.

After one lap, Deena settled in a few feet behind Carly, Sasha, and Monique. A lot of the other girls clearly hadn't run this summer. They were slogging around the track, gasping for breath. Carly's stride was smooth and graceful. As Deena kept her eyes on the three of them, she noticed Sasha and Monique were huffing and puffing. Their chests were rising and falling nearly twice as fast as Carly's.

Deena was not at all tired, but she had no intention of sprinting out ahead of them. Doing that would be social suicide. She wanted to do well without calling much attention to herself.

As the second lap ended—Mr. Humphries called out a time of 2:57—Sasha and Monique began drifting backward. Carly held her pace. Deena held hers—a few feet back. She did not make eye contact with either Sasha or Monique as she passed them. But she could hear how heavily they were breathing. She could still hear them, desperately holding onto a fast pace, as they drifted in the space behind her.

As Deena hit the top of the stretch on the third lap, she decided to put on a burst of speed to close the gap on Carly. She didn't pull even with her, but remained a half step behind, just off Carly's right shoulder. She knew Carly knew she was right there, although Carly—a seasoned runner—did not turn over her shoulder to look.

The pair crossed the starting line within a half step of each other. Deena saw that Mr. Humphries was smiling, although she couldn't be sure if the smile was for her or if he was just glaring into the sun.

"4:28," he called out as they zoomed past.

Deena could run whatever pace Carly decided to set. And she did just that, making no effort to pass Carly, but casually extending her stride whenever Carly extended hers. Through the 100-yard mark, and into the far turn, Deena stayed exactly half a step behind. She knew she would not try to win the race. She knew that staying exactly where she was said more than any victory could.

As they cruised around the final turn, Carly went into a sprint. Deena joined her, knowing everyone on the track was watching each stride.

She—Deena Jackson!—was, for once, the center of attention. And she liked it. The feeling was as good as she'd always imagined it might be.

The sun was bright in the sky. Deena could feel the eyes of the other girls on her, and she could hear her own rapid breathing inside of her head. It was a tiring final lap. Carly crossed in 5:35, one second ahead of Deena, which was just the way Deena wanted it.

The two girls slowed to a walk as they waited for everyone else to finish. Sasha and Monique were not too far behind, finishing in 6:15.

Deena walked in the area just past the finish line, hands on hips. She fought the urge to bend over her toes or raise her arms in the air. She tried to control her breathing, despite feeling as if her lungs were trying to break free from her chest. She did not want Carly to believe she'd exerted any energy. Carly walked the same area, hands locked behind her head. Sasha and Monique soon joined their friend, and the three of them walked onto the infield grass.

Deena walked in the opposite direction and lifted her heel to the short chain-link fence. She leaned forward and stretched her hamstrings.

A minute later, Mr. Humphries called, "Bring it in! Everyone!" Deena jogged over to the infield grass and took a seat behind a group of freshmen.

"Interesting day," he began, looking directly at Deena. She instinctively dropped her eyes. "If you just finished your mile, please do at least one cool-down lap. Everyone else, meet here tomorrow morning at 10."

Deena slowly jogged home. Although she felt tired from the workout, she was propelled by her excitement to tell her dad about the first day.

When she walked in the front door, Deena was surprised, and happy, to see Jamal sitting on the couch next to Dad. Jamal was sitting as close as possible to the recliner and reading out loud from the newspaper. Deena recognized the words as that morning's recap of the Phillies' victory the night before.

When they spotted her, Jamal lowered the paper. He seemed to shrug at his sister, acknowledging both her presence and what he'd been doing for Dad.

"So?" Dad asked, turning slowly to look at Deena.

"It went really well," Deena said, striding into the room and sitting next to her brother on the couch. She told them both about her morning, giving the minute-by-minute breakdown of everything except the snubs from her teammates.

The next day, the team went for a long pack run. They ran for just about an hour and then stretched on the grass afterward. Deena continued to stay just behind Carly and whoever else ran with Carly. There were no timed races on either Tuesday or Wednesday. But on Thursday, Mr. Humphries announced that there would be a scrimmage distance race the next day. All ages and teams were supposed to meet at 11 a.m. in Fairmount Park, home of the school's cross-country course.

Friday's practice would be a scrimmage 5K, the exact distance of varsity cross-country races. Mr. Humphries said the race would "go a long way" toward deciding the teams.

On Friday morning, Deena awoke much earlier than she'd hoped. She had set her alarm for 9 a.m., but found herself fidgeting in her bed just after 7. She rolled from one side to the other, hugging her pillow, willing herself back to sleep. But her muscles and mind were nervous about the 5K.

After a few minutes, she heard the low volume of the living-room TV. She knew that meant her dad was awake. Deena pulled a t-shirt over her head and slipped on her flip-flops before trudging out to the living room. "I can't sleep," she said when her dad turned to look at her.

His face had melted down to the thinness of a candle. Once robust and full, he looked as if he could slip through a crack in the floor. Deena didn't want to think about his cancer, so she willed herself to think about something else: today's practice race.

"It's the timed 5K this morning," she said, sitting Indian-style on the couch next to her dad and making sure to keep her spine straight and not slump forward.

"I know, honey. I've been thinking about it all morning."

"You have?"

"Why do you think I'm awake so early?"

"Because you're restless all the time now?"

"That, too," he smiled, but his smile was like a burned-out bulb. "It feels like my bones are poking into me . . ." He paused for a second. "Baby girl, would you mind getting me one of those yogurts the doctor says I should try to eat?"

"Of course." She jumped off the couch and went into the kitchen, calling back to him, "Where's Mom?"

"Shhhh," he said. "She's trying to get some sleep before my appointment."

"Sorry." She handed him the opened yogurt and a spoon. As he grasped the silver handle, Deena noticed the oval end of the spoon shaking. In her dad's hand, the spoon looked like an anchor. She looked away.

"How are things with your teammates?" he asked. "Have you made any friends? You only talk about the running."

"They've all been friends for years," she said as she plopped back onto the couch.

"What does that mean?"

"It means I'm sure they all wish I'd disappear."

"Oh, baby girl." He lowered the spoon into the yogurt and let the cup rest on the recliner's arm. "It'll just take them a little while, that's all."

"No, it's awful." She was surprised by the forcefulness of her response. "They hate me. It'll never change."

Her father sighed, and Deena began watching the TV as if nothing was more interesting than the morning news.

• • •

A few hours later, Deena walked slowly to Fairmount Park. She hadn't slept enough the night before, and now she regretted not staying in bed longer. The day's warmth was lulling her toward a nap. She yawned as she stepped onto the curb and walked along the sidewalk bordering the park.

Nothing was right this morning. Her mom had been on edge when she finally awoke and helped her father to the car for his appointment; Jamal never came out of his room, which was getting to be a recurring theme; and she had snapped at her dad when he tried to give her advice about making friends on the team.

"Just keep trying," he had said that morning. "They're going to come around."

Deena had still been sitting on the couch, pretending to watch the TV, when he pressed ahead. "I remember when I tried out for the high school football team," he continued. "They hazed me the entire first month. I had to sing out loud at the first team dinner, and I was always forced to carry the equipment from the bus."

"Dad," she had cut him off. "That's not even remotely what's happening with me. You don't even know what you're talking about. These girls aren't hazing me; they just don't want me on the team at all." She had stood up then and left the living room.

Why couldn't she just let her dad say whatever he wanted to say, whatever he thought might help?

Deena kicked a stone and watched it skip into the grass. She didn't want to run today. She wanted to go back home, curl up in bed, and cry until her dad returned from his chemo appointment.

As Deena waited for Mr. Humphries to start the 5K trial, she thought maybe her body would surprise her. She felt worn down and tired, yes; but maybe once she began running, the opposite would be true.

She was wrong.

Within the first 100 yards, which was a stretch of field before the course narrowed and entered the woods, Deena knew she was in trouble. It felt as if she was running uphill, although she knew she wasn't. Her legs felt heavy, and her lungs gasped for air. What was even more depressing for Deena was that as she watched Carly stride out in front of her, she felt no desire to catch her.

Each step of the race was painful. Deena couldn't stop thinking about what she'd said to her dad. During one moment midway through, while deep in the woods with no one surrounding her, she felt a choking cry rise from her chest and into her throat. She allowed it to escape from her body in the form of dripping tears as she continued running. She refused to stop, walk, or look behind her. It was her first true test in her running career. She'd never felt so defeated. But would she quit?

She wouldn't quit. She *couldn't*. She kept her eyes on each curve in the woods. Her sneakers crunched twigs and avoided dips, and she felt grateful for the seclusion of the trees. Carly was too far ahead to worry about catching, and Monique and Sasha had passed her before the first mile marker. It had been disappointing to see them push past her, but now that felt like so long ago. Like it was another race entirely.

It was underneath the shade of the trees that Deena realized this wasn't a contest against other runners. It was a contest against herself.

Without slowing, she took a few deep breaths against her thudding heart and tried to calm her breathing. She wiped her eyes clean of any tears and lifted her head to watch each turn ahead. A breeze blew through the tree trunks and felt good against her face and legs. She knew she was running out of the cross-country course, and that was fine with her.

At last, the final bend of the woods showed a burst of light. All that was left was the final straightaway that funneled into the finish line. She was into the clearing and could see the dots of people near the finish line: Mr. Humphries, Carly, probably Monique and Sasha.

Deena kept her pace through multiple softball fields until those at the finish line came into focus. Each one became larger with each step.

It was almost over. Her legs felt wobbly with fatigue.

Mr. Humphries, clipboard in one hand, stopwatch in the other, watched her as she crossed the finish line. He called out her time, "21:45," and then scribbled onto his board.

Deena pulled to an immediate stop and fell over her knees, gasping for breath. Her chest was heaving up and down, more with the emotion of the day than anything else. *It's over, it's over, I made it,* she said to herself. *I finished.*

As other runners began to trickle in behind her, Deena lifted herself off the ground and began walking to her gear, just a few yards away. The sun was quickly drying the sweat on her brow, turning it into a salt line. She could hear Carly, Monique, and Sasha cheering on the other girls.

"Come on, ladies!" Carly's voice rang out behind her, followed by clapping. "You got this, just a few more yards! Finish strong!"

Deena lowered herself to her small patch of grass. Her water bottle rested between her flip-flops, next to the t-shirt she'd worn over her runner's singlet. She extended her legs in front of her and stretched her hamstrings.

The encouragement and cheering continued near the finish line. Some of the girls, just freshmen, would take another ten minutes to finish the course. Deena closed her eyes and concentrated on lowering her heart rate. After a minute of deep breathing, she finally felt in control of herself, her body, and her emotions. She lifted the water bottle. The slivers of ice—what had once been ice cubes from her freezer—sloshed in the water. She twisted off the top and gulped the cooling water. It dripped down her chin and onto her singlet.

She didn't care.

Just then, a pair of sneakers came into the space by her feet. Deena looked up to see

Monique towering over her. Monique had her hands on her hips. One corner of her lip was raised, and her head was tilted sideways.

"You're not as good as you thought, huh?"

Carly appeared from behind Monique and watched for Deena's response. Deena said nothing. She glanced between the two girls standing over her, first at Monique, then at Carly, and then she lowered her eyes into her water bottle. The slivers of ice had melted entirely into the water.

Deena felt tears welling in her eyes. She did not look up.

"What's wrong with you, girl?" Carly said.

Deena barely raised her eyes, risking more ridicule. She was surprised to see Carly's attention turned toward Monique, her hand gripping Monique's arm.

"What?" Monique seemed genuinely confused.

"It's enough, OK?" Carly said, pulling her friend away from Deena.

Deena watched as the two of them turned, Monique more surprised than anything. They were walking away. Carly was still holding Monique's arm when she glanced over her shoulder at Deena.

Neither said anything. Neither blinked. They just made eye contact for an extended second, and then Carly turned away.

Chapter 6

Deena made the varsity.

She'd never finished worse than fourth in any practice race, so her inclusion on the varsity team was no surprise, although she still took pleasure in hearing Mr. Humphries call her name as a member of the team. Perhaps it was a small victory that none of the other varsity girls said anything—good or bad—about her selection.

The team's first meet was on the Saturday after the first week of school. Early Saturday morning, Deena needed a ride to the team bus. She awoke before dawn, pulled on her sweats, packed her bag, and walked out to the living room. She was surprised to find her dad jingling his car keys.

"Where are you going?" she asked.

"I'm taking you to the bus."

"You are? Are you sure? Do you feel OK?"

His clothes hung on him as if on a wire hanger, but his face and eyes had more life and excitement than she'd seen in weeks. It had been a great week. On Thursday, he'd gone for his monthly cell-count update at the hospital, and the news had been remarkable: the cancer's progression seemed to have stalled.

Last night, in celebration, the family had gone to Outback Steakhouse, where they'd always gone for birthdays and special events. Although exhausted from the evening, Dad had stayed awake for the 90 minutes of dinner, even finishing an entire sweet potato and poking at everyone else's steaks. He had drifted asleep on the way home, but so what? The entire family had been buoyed by the streak of normality.

Now, he stood in the living room prepared to give her a ride, just as he'd always done. "I feel good, baby girl. And, it's your first race!" he said. "I wish I could go, but the doc says that's just too much. Soon, though, I'll be there."

She smiled at the thought and said, "You ready?"

He nodded, and Deena grabbed his arm and led him outside toward his truck. She braced him outside the driver's side door as he labored to lift himself into the seat. It was a slow process, but he was moving much better than she'd seen. When he was settled, she darted around to the passenger's seat and climbed next to him.

"My girl's first race," he said as he started the engine. "Who would have thought?"

"Not me," she laughed.

"I always thought you could be a runner."

"You did?"

"When you were little, you'd scamper all over the park. You had these long, athletic legs, and I remember saying to your mom once, 'She's going to be a runner.'"

"What happened?"

"You got into your books," he laughed, shrugging. "And you forgot about everything else."

"I guess I did," Deena said.

"There are worse things to get into," he continued. "At least that's what your mom always consoled me with."

"You were upset?"

"Not upset, no. I just thought you had some of my athletic prowess in you. I always thought I could be a part of that, if you got into sports."

Deena thought about this for a minute, staring out the rearview mirror as the street passed behind her. Finally, she said, "I never knew that."

"So, today's race," he continued, as if unwilling for the conversation to become more emotional. "Do you have a game plan?"

"Yes, actually, I do."

"What is it?" He turned his head slightly toward her, splitting his attention between the road and Deena.

"I want to win. That's my plan."

Her dad laughed, although his laughter quickly evolved into a cough. It took him a second to recover. "OK, baby girl," he finally said. "Then win it."

The meet was in Lower Merion, one of the nicest suburbs of Philadelphia.

Deena sat in the front row of the bus, her eyes glued to the window. Mr. Humphries sat across the row, buried in a book he was reading. She knew the trip was short—the school was only 20 minutes from Ben Franklin—but it felt to her as if she was leaving her comfort zone. It was her first cross-country meet. It was her first race. It was her first athletic competition.

She might as well be traveling to another state. Every few minutes, a flurry of nerves washed through her stomach.

The bus bumped along the highway before exiting to the lush side streets of Lower Merion. She had never been there before, but she marveled at the landscaped yards and storybook houses lining the shaded streets. Just when she was considering pulling out her book, the bus took a sharp left into the school complex. Up ahead were a dozen other yellow buses, all parked to the side. Covering the grass were dozens of colored tents and hundreds of kids walking and running in their school colors. It looked as if a bag of Skittles—red, yellow, orange, purple— had been tossed onto the school's grounds.

Ben Franklin's bus pulled up to the curb, and the doors opened. Deena grabbed her bag and stood up. As she stepped into the aisle of the bus, she caught Mr. Humphries' eye. He motioned for her to sit down next to him. She slipped across the aisle and planted herself on the edge of the seat.

The rest of the girls filed off the bus. Deena made an effort to keep her eyes down in case some of the varsity girls—they always sat at the very back of the bus—were trying to give her dirty looks for sitting next to the coach.

When the bus was empty, Mr. Humphries

spoke. "What are you reading these days?"

It wasn't the question she thought he wanted to ask, but she pulled out a copy of the library book, which was required summer reading, and showed it to him: "*To Kill a Mockingbird.*"

"Ah," he said, "that's a good one." He flipped *his* book over, revealing the title: *Water for Elephants.* He seemed embarrassed by the selection, adding, "My friend begged me to read it. I guess the movie is coming out next week."

"Looks fun to me," Deena said, noting the bright colors on the front.

They sat for a second without saying anything. The driver maneuvered the bus into the parking lot and pulled on the emergency brake. He offered Mr. Humphries a slight wave as he walked down the bus's three steps.

"So, Deena, I wanted to talk to you about something," Mr. Humphries began.

"OK . . ."

"It's about college."

"Oh, OK, what about college?" Deena had no idea what to say to him about this subject. She hadn't even yet talked to her parents.

"I received a call yesterday from the guidance counselor, and she mentioned that you didn't sign up for an application appointment."

That was true. All seniors considering applying to college were encouraged to take advantage of the guidance center's advice. The deadline for making an appointment had been Friday. As she had all summer, Deena had intended to talk to her parents last week. But each day had passed, and the time just never seemed right. She had missed the deadline.

"Things have just been so busy," she offered as an excuse.

"Does that mean you're planning on applying?"

She delayed by stuffing her book back into her backpack. "I'm not sure yet," she said.

"Not sure?" He shifted in his seat so that he was facing her directly. "You've been my best English student for three years. I always assumed you were headed to college. What happened?"

Deena looked down, unsure of what to say.

Mr. Humphries put a hand on her shoulder and waited for her to collect her thoughts. Finally, when it became clear to him that she wasn't going to say anything, he said, "How can I help?"

Deena clasped her hands together and watched the veins protrude from her skin. She looked at her legs and flexed the quad muscle that was now sinewy and developed. She was surprised when the first tear dropped from her eyes and landed on the top of her white sneaker. A second tear covered the first, and a third covered the second. They plopped onto her sneakers, and she watched each of them land.

Mr. Humphries tried again. "What is it?"

Deena hadn't spoken with anyone outside her family about what was happening. It wasn't anyone else's burden, and she didn't want to turn her dad's cancer into her own pity party. She didn't want to accept someone's condolences; it would be too much like accepting payment for something she didn't want to sell. Somewhere inside her, she felt as if crying and complaining about the raw hand they'd been dealt would only accelerate the cancer.

Maybe this is ridiculous, she thought. *Maybe I'm holding inside something that needs to be released.*

Deena waited until the tears stopped falling. Then she sat up straight and looked at Mr. Humphries. Behind his reading glasses, his eyes were focused, concerned. His mouth was turned downward. He was waiting for her to speak.

"My dad is sick," she exhaled. "Everything's different now."

He gripped his book with both hands, but did not lose eye contact. "Tell me," he said. "What's happening?"

She shook her head slowly, "It's bad, it's cancer, and it's the worst kind. I don't know what's going to happen, but everything is different. I kept meaning to talk to my parents about next year, but it's like they just forgot about it. It's like they forgot about everything that's supposed to happen . . . afterward. I don't know."

"Is that . . . do you think that's why you started running?"

"Yes."

"Give me two minutes." He stood up and slid out of the seat past her, hustling down the stairs and outside to where the rest of the girls had gathered.

Deena watched as Mr. Humphries gave them instructions about where to pitch the tent and who was scheduled for their warm-up run, and when they were scheduled. The first race— the freshman race—was still an hour away.

He was back in two minutes.

The bus baked in the sunlight, but Mr. Humphries made no move to leave. They talked about the past three months: the cancer, school, running, and the future. In the end, he made Deena promise that she would speak with her parents that night.

She gave him a quick hug and grabbed her backpack. She felt lighter.

"Do you remember what I said to you at the end of last year?"

She gripped the straps of her backpack. Of course she remembered. "Yes," she said. "You said, 'Don't fade into the background just because it feels easiest.'"

Mr. Humphries smiled.

"Right," he said. "And that's especially true today."

The varsity race was the last one of the day. Deena had spent hours listening to music on her phone, stretching, warming up, and watching the freshman and junior varsity races. It was cool in the shade of the team's tent, and at one point she even closed her eyes and pictured the course, each turn she would make, each stretch during which she could build speed.

When the race coordinator finally called the varsity girls to the starting line, Deena felt calm and confident. She followed Mr. Humphries and her four teammates to the starting line. There, perched along a white line spray-painted into the grass, stood at least a hundred other runners.

The announcer issued a two-minute warning. Deena took off her t-shirt and gym shorts, revealing Ben Franklin's cross-country uniform: a tiny singlet and spandex. She hopped twice to stretch her muscles and waited for Mr. Humphries' instructions.

"Nobody go out too fast," he cautioned. "It's the first race, so we're not sure what to expect. I want everyone to gradually push herself, and we'll see what we've got this season. This is the starting point."

The announcer, bugle to mouth, called the one-minute warning.

"Bring it together," Mr. Humphries said, thrusting his hand into the middle of the circle. Each of the girls followed until their arms and hands made a wheel.

"Ben Franklin on three: one, two, three . . ."
"Ben Franklin!"

This was a runner's high, Deena thought to herself as she cruised through the first two miles. She kept herself in the lead pack of five girls. Carly was to her right, keeping pace.

Deena knew she would win. She felt as if she was jogging, not racing, as the course wound along grassy straights, up one hill, through a man-made path along the back of the school property. Just after passing the two-mile marker, they ran to the side of the school's baseball diamond. It was empty, with patches of grass poking through on the pitcher's mound and near first base.

They curved around the backstop, and Deena shifted gears. With just about one mile left, she was prepared to blister that final mile. She would force the other four girls to run her pace. She opened her stride and injected life into her arms. Two of the girls stayed with her for the first two minutes. But they soon trailed off, falling back to what was now the secondary pack.

The final section of the course funneled the runners onto the school's track. They finished with one lap on the dusty red surface. Deena was curious to glance behind her and see exactly where the other girls were. But she knew she wouldn't give them that hope.

Mr. Humphries was on the backstretch of the track, holding his clipboard. As she whizzed past him, he gave her a thumbs up and nodded his head.

Deena increased her speed with each step. By the final 100 yards, she felt as if she was sprinting a 400 instead of finishing a 5K. She was floating along as she crossed the finish line. She had won, and she felt as if she had so much left inside of her.

She slowly pulled to a stop. The race's volunteers, who took down her bib number, congratulated her on the race. "You look like you could run another," said an older woman, handing her a cup of water. "Great job."

Deena smiled at the woman and then turned to watch the next finishers. Carly was on the final stretch, and Deena watched as she kicked to the finish line. Carly finished third and did not look as if she could have run another race.

Deena looked around at the parents and friends lining the track's fence. She couldn't wait to tell her dad about the race. She wished she had her cell phone with her at that very moment. He would be so proud.

As she sipped from the paper cup, Deena felt a sweaty arm across her shoulder. Carly, chest heaving, was leaning against her. "Great race," Carly puffed. "You were awesome."

Deena had no idea how to respond. She

finally managed a "Thank you," looking awkwardly at the girl draped across her shoulder.

Mr. Humphries appeared in front of them, having jogged across the track. "You guys were great!" he said, spreading his arms wide. "Incredible race!"

"Thanks," Deena responded, looking down at the tops of her sneakers.

Carly squeezed her shoulder once and then removed her arm. "We're going to walk back to the tent and then go for a cool-down," she said.

Deena had to stop herself from saying, "We are?"

Mr. Humphries' eyebrows rose slightly, but he motioned with his clipboard as if excusing them from his presence. He caught Deena's eye and winked as the two of them passed.

Deena widened her eyes and shrugged.

Inside the tent, Carly rummaged through her backpack. Finally she stood, a black t-shirt in one hand. She was pulling it over her head when Monique and Sasha returned to the tent.

"Girls!" Carly said. "We were just coming to get you."

Deena glanced from Carly to her friends. Neither girl seemed comforted by Carly's declaration that they had been on their way to find them. Monique tilted her head slightly and said, "Oh, yeah? You were going to come back for us?" Monique's long nails, painted bold red, were perched on her hips, her entire body waiting for a response.

Deena stepped away from the tent, removing herself from whatever interaction the three of them were about to engage in. She walked far enough away that she could no longer hear what was being said. She sat on the grass and stretched, waiting for Carly and whoever else might join the cool-down.

A few minutes later, Carly emerged from the tent alone. Deena wasn't surprised. She stood up from the grass and watched Carly approach: long, slender, athletic, her quad muscles sinewy.

"We're ready," said Carly. And Deena was surprised to see Sasha and Monique emerge from the tent, looking like scolded sidekicks. They approached slowly, if not completely unwillingly.

The four of them set off on a slow jog away from the tents and cross-country course, which was empty in advance of the boys' varsity race. Carly pulled alongside Deena, while Sasha and Monique drifted behind.

Neither of them said anything for the first few minutes. Deena felt cooled by the breeze that was collecting in the trees and brushing across them. For the first half mile, there was no sound between them except for their sneakers hitting the ground.

"So," Carly finally said. "Let's talk . . ."

Deena kept her eyes ahead. "OK," she said, goose bumps forming on her arms.

"I'm really glad you tried out for the team," Carly began.

Deena smiled to herself and whispered, "Me too."

"It took a lot of courage to show up that first day," said Carly.

"I don't know," Deena replied. "It's probably something I should have done a couple of years ago."

"You think?" Carly sounded surprised.

"Yeah, my dad always said I could be a runner, but . . ."

For a second, Carly waited for Deena to continue, but she didn't. "But . . . what?" Carly nudged.

"But, well, you've seen me at school." Deena lowered her voice so it could barely be heard above the cracking of twigs underfoot. "I didn't want to risk it."

Carly seemed to think about this for a minute. Just when Deena assumed she wasn't going to reply at all, Carly spoke. "I guess I always thought you didn't mind being by yourself."

"Really? You thought that?"

"You always seemed fine just reading a book or studying."

"Huh," Deena said, but she didn't say anything else.

For the next twenty minutes, they talked about running. They talked about school. They talked about Carly's plans for college. Deena learned exactly why Carly had been chosen captain of all the school's running teams. She was more mature than those initial interactions indicated.

"I'm sorry about how this started," Carly said. "I know it doesn't make sense, but sometimes it's hard when someone comes in and takes someone else's place." She glanced quickly backward, toward Sasha and Monique. "It's been just the three of us for so many years. And I guess we wanted to keep it that way. I know it might not make sense to you."

Deena just nodded, glad for the conversation, even thrilled by it, and slightly worried she might say the wrong thing if she said anything at all.

When the afternoon was in its final few minutes, the team boarded the yellow school bus.

Despite the friendly turn the day had taken, Deena slipped into the bus's front seat. She didn't want to push her luck by showing up in the rear seats. Mr. Humphries slid into the seat across from her, and the two of them watched as the bus filled first with freshmen and sophomores, and then juniors and seniors.

Carly boarded the bus, headphones covering her ears, and smiled as she passed Deena. Sasha and Monique boarded last and scooted past Deena, stepping down the aisle without making eye contact.

That's OK, Deena said to herself, thinking she'd had enough victories for one day. But then Monique reappeared, and Deena lifted her eyes up and looked at her.

"Nice race," Monique said.

"Thank you," Deena heard herself respond.

Deena pulled out her headphones and plugged them into her phone, hoping to listen to music on the ride home. She touched the phone's dark screen, expecting it to brighten. Nothing happened. She held down the power button, and the outline of an empty battery flashed quickly on the screen.

The phone was dead. She shouldn't have listened to so much music all day. That drained the battery faster than anything else.

Wrapping the white headphones around the dead phone, Deena shoved it back into the pocket of her backpack. She leaned her head against the glass window and pictured telling her father about today's race—about everything that had happened today. She couldn't help smiling to herself.

When the bus rolled to a stop in front of the high school, Deena jumped off and scanned the streets for her dad's truck.

He wasn't there. She felt a flutter of unease in her stomach as she looked at her watch: 5:12. The bus had been twelve minutes later than predicted. She looked down the street at the oncoming traffic, hoping maybe she'd see him approaching. Then she walked over to the school's steps—the ones on which they'd held that first cross-country meeting—

and sank onto the first step. From there, she could see the oncoming traffic in both directions.

Deena watched as all the girls climbed into cars or began walking home. Carly ducked into the backseat of an old brown Buick, waving a quick goodbye to Deena before she disappeared behind the tinted windows.

Soon, Deena was alone on the steps. With each passing second, her nerves became more frayed. She began rubbing her palms against the tops of her knees, watching each wave of oncoming traffic that came into view.

A Honda Accord pulled up in front of the school. The passenger's side window rolled down. Deena recognized Mr. Humphries leaning across the seat. She walked to the window and peered inside.

"You need a ride?"

"I don't know. Someone was supposed to be here at 5." She looked at the street as if giving it one final shot.

"I'll give you a ride home."

Deena knew she needed to get home as soon as possible. It would take her an hour to walk home. Her parents were never late. Her parents never just forgot to collect one of their kids. She opened the door and gave Mr. Humphries her address as she got inside.

"Something wrong?"

"Yes," she said. "No. Well, maybe. I think so. I'm worried. I have a bad feeling." She turned to him. "Could you hurry? I'm sorry. My phone died on the bus, so I don't know what's happening."

In response, Mr. Humphries pressed on the gas and took a quick left turn ahead of oncoming traffic. He proved himself an expert in hustle driving: he timed the lights perfectly and had her home in twelve minutes, which for Philly's city streets was a remarkable time.

Swinging open the car door, Deena thanked him. She heard his request for a phone call later, but shut the door before responding. She was inside her house in three long strides, pushing herself through the front door and hoping desperately that she'd find her dad in his recliner. Even though something in her heart told her this was a ridiculous hope, she was still crushed to find the recliner empty. She peered into the kitchen while flying down the hallway and pushing open doors.

All the rooms were empty.

Deena came back into the kitchen and

dropped her bag by the table. It was then she noticed the note on the kitchen counter. She recognized her mother's handwriting, but only barely. The note was obviously quickly written, and Deena could sense the panic in the hastily formed words.

> **Deena, tried calling you. Going to hospital—emergency. Call cell as soon as home. Sorry, Mom."**

A knock at the front door ripped her away from the note. Mr. Humphries was standing behind the screen, a few steps from the door, as if he was worried he'd frighten her if he stood too close. He lifted his thumb in the direction of his car, which was still parked along the curb. "I thought maybe you needed a ride?"

Deena looked into the space between Mr. Humphries and his car. She was looking past it all.

"Yes," she said finally, stepping forward and pulling the door closed behind her. "I have to go to the hospital."

Chapter 7

They made the decision that Dad would be cared for at home. Deena pretended not to know what this meant, while Jamal seemed actually not to know.

Deena had arrived at the hospital the night before, fearful of what she might find. She ended up walking slowly into her father's room as if it might be the room of a stranger. *Would he be awake? Would he look different? Would he be scared?* Her mom had relayed what had happened just a few hours beforehand: his liver had been in the initial stages of failing. They had hustled him to the hospital, so he wasn't in immediate jeopardy, but the doctor had explained that this was the start. And Deena understood this meant the start of something they'd all rather avoid. It was the start of the end.

She walked into the room, still wearing her running sneakers and her cross-country uniform under her t-shirt. Dad was tucked underneath the white sheets, and Deena couldn't help comparing him to the last time she'd seen him in one of these beds: he was half his former size. She remembered him months ago, looking like a giant draped across a baby bed. On this night he looked like a small child tucked into a king-size bed.

Deena exhaled slowly and wiped away the tears that had welled up in her eyes. Her mom caught sight of her in the doorway and softly waved her inside. Except for the steady beeping of the machine connected to her dad, the room was still. Jamal sat in a chair in the corner. He had headphones in his ears, and his eyes were glued to his iPod.

Deena entered the room as if everything in it were breakable, careful to avoid the corner of the bed and the side table. She stood behind her mom's chair, which was pulled as close to the bed as possible. She placed her hands on her mom's shoulders. The muscles immediately melted beneath Deena's hands as if they hadn't been touched in years. Deena thought she heard a soft whimper escape her mom's lips, but she pretended not to notice.

Her mom put her hand on top of Deena's hand, and they stayed like that for a long while. The spell was interrupted by Dad, who coughed himself awake. His eyes flashed open: deep brown pupils with a curtain pulled halfway across. He struggled to keep his eyes open. But then his gaze focused on Deena, and he seemed to remember something important. He tried to lift himself higher in the bed. The effort was futile. He sank back into the prone position.

Mom turned and looked over her shoulder, patting Deena's hand. She nodded her head as encouragement.

"I won the race," Deena said aloud, cutting through the room's silence.

After saying those words, Deena instinctively stood taller. She searched her dad's face for understanding, but his eyes were closed. She watched his lips, cracked and dried. A twitching started at the corner of his mouth, and she watched as a smile slowly crept across his face. It wasn't the wide, world-beating smile she remembered, but it was still his smile. Then he opened his eyes, and Deena saw that they were shining. She let go of her mom's shoulders and dropped to her knees next to the bed. She grabbed his hand and squeezed it to let him know she was there.

Deena and Carly shared top honors throughout the season. In most league races, Carly and Deena finished first and second. The order was dependent on who excelled that particular day, but regardless of which one finished first, the two of them always jogged their cool-down together, as they had after that first race. While allowing their muscles to unwind, they talked about the race: the hardest point, how they'd felt, what they could do differently next time. By the time they boarded the bus home, Deena always felt as if she'd learned something for her next race.

Carly had even asked for Deena's cell phone number, a moment that had made Deena's heart skip a beat. When Carly's first text message had lit up Deena's phone—*Great race today, girl, get some rest!*—Deena had spent the rest of the evening with a stupid grin on her face. After texting her response—*Thanks! You did so well, too. Guess we both need our rest today!*—she found herself checking her phone every few minutes to see if Carly had written again.

As the season progressed, Carly sent Deena more text messages, usually after practices or races. Deena loved having a reason to check her phone; it put a bounce in her step.

The Ben Franklin cross-country team ran undefeated through league play and competed well during weekend invitationals. The races often included more than 40 teams and more than 200 runners in each race.

But as Deena's running improved, her father's health declined.

Then, one evening, his blood pressure plummeted. It was the night before Philly's public school championship, the race that would qualify Ben Franklin to compete for the State Championships. The sound of the beeping machinery yanked Deena from a light sleep. She startled awake and darted down the hallway into the living room.

The white sheets, the overhead light, and the medical devices' electronic screens seemed to make the bed glow. The nurses were huddled around her dad, pulling and prodding, while her mother was holding his hand.

Deena felt Jamal beside her. He pressed his shoulder into hers.

"What's happening?" he asked.

"I don't know," she responded—because she didn't.

One of the nurses caught Deena's eye and nodded once, gesturing back down the hallway. Deena nodded in response.

"Let's wait back here," she said, walking toward Jamal's room.

They sat on his bed, which was still warm from his body heat. "This sucks," Jamal said, dropping his head into his hands.

"Yeah, it kind of does."

"What are we supposed to do?"

"There's nothing we can do."

"We just sit here—that's it?"

Deena took a deep breath and said, "Yeah, I think that's it."

The two of them sat quietly, listening as machines continued beeping and the nurses barked orders. Deena reached for Jamal's knee and let her hand rest there. A few minutes later, there was a knock at the door. Their mom, followed closely by one of the nurses, nudged her way into the room.

"Hey babies," she said, her face ashen. "We just wanted to explain to you everything that's happening."

The nurse gently touched Candice's arm and stepped into the room.

When the nurse finished, Candice asked the question Deena wouldn't have asked because she didn't want to seem insensitive in the face of such despair.

"Do you think Deena should go to her race tomorrow?"

The nurse grimaced, as if she was pained to deliver the verdict.

"I don't know; nobody knows," she said, speaking slowly. "But, my experience tells me that tomorrow could be a difficult day. The decision is yours to make."

It had been a long night, but in the morning, Dad's breathing and heart rate had stabilized. Deena had sat next to the monstrous hospital bed, which now filled every open space of their living room, and watched the screen that displayed her dad's heart rate. She was amazed that the same measurement she used as an athletic threshold could determine, for her dad, something entirely different.

Deena thought about that day's race: the Philly public school championships. She could almost feel the crisp autumn air, the excitement and energy, as all of the city's runners prepared for the season's most important race. Ben Franklin needed to finish in the top three to qualify for states. Could the team do that without her?

Deena sat up on the couch and dropped her head between her knees. She took a few deep breaths and told herself everything would be OK. And when the sun began spilling through the windows, Deena walked over to the house telephone and dialed Mr. Humphries' home number.

Mr. Humphries picked up on the third ring. "Hello," he said, sounding more alert than he should have been so early in the morning.

"Hi, Coach," she said. "It's Deena."

"Deena, are you OK?"

"Yeah . . . well . . . kind of." She stared out into the backyard. "It was a rough night."

"How is he?"

"Not good."

Mr. Humphries didn't say anything. He waited.

"I can't run today. I'm sorry. I just can't leave him."

"Of course, of course, absolutely—you need to stay there. I'll talk to the team as soon as everyone is on the . . ."

"No," Deena interrupted. "I mean . . . no, please don't do that. Please don't tell them."

"Why not?"

Deena thought about this. She looked down at the tops of her feet. It didn't make sense. But it was how she felt. "I don't want them to feel sorry for me."

Reluctantly, Mr. Humphries agreed not to tell her teammates. But he warned her that they would be disappointed by her absence, especially without an explanation.

She told him she'd figure it out later.

"Don't put off until tomorrow what you can do today," he told her just before hanging up the phone.

Deena had dropped the receiver, slightly annoyed that he was still trying to teach her, even in a time like this. She walked into the living room and slumped onto the couch. She closed her eyes and, without even trying to, fell asleep next to her dad.

A few hours later, Deena awoke to the sound of her cell phone ringing. She looked down at the touch screen: Carly. She silenced the phone, only to find a number of texts from earlier.

"*Where are u?*"

"Coach told us ur not coming. I can't believe ur not here today."

"Is everything OK?"

"Please, call me as soon as u can."

Deena got up from the couch, walked down the hallway into her bedroom, and pulled open the top drawer of her dresser. She looked once more at the phone, then slipped it underneath a layer of clothes and closed the drawer.

The next day, Deena awoke before the sun, threw on a pair of sweats, and walked out into the frosty morning air up to the end of her driveway. She looked left, then right, until she spotted what she wanted. Three driveways down, she knelt and picked up the morning newspaper, still wrapped in plastic. She slipped the tightly rolled paper out of the bag and removed the rubber band.

Even though her body still felt heated from the bed's warmth, Deena's teeth began chattering. She flipped through the sections until she found "Sports." Glancing at the index, she then peeled through the first few pages until she found the coverage of Saturday's meet. She squinted at the small print, which listed the teams' order of finish. Her heart skipped a beat as she found the listing for the girls' race.

Ben Franklin had finished third! They'd qualified for states!

Deena felt lighter. She allowed a small smile to creep across her lips. Next, she found the individual results and noticed that Monique had run her best time of the year.

She let out a long sigh, her warm breath meeting the cold air and forming what looked like a puff of smoke. She returned the sports section to its proper place, rolled the paper tightly, and slipped it back into the plastic. Then she dropped the paper at her feet and walked back to her house.

The night before the state championship meet, a team dinner was to be held at Carly's house. Deena's mom and the nurses convinced Deena that she should go to the dinner. They assured her that her dad was stable enough for the time being.

Deena refused and excused herself to her bedroom. She curled herself into the corner chair and lifted her book. She stared at the same page, rereading it a dozen times without absorbing a word. Stubbornly, she refused to drop the book from her gaze.

Then a slight knock came at her door.

Before Deena could say anything, the door opened, and her mom peeked around the frame. "Honey," she said. "Can I come in?"

Deena nodded her response. Her mom carried the desk chair to the corner, and the two sat very near one another. Mom clasped her hands together and dangled them between her legs. She tilted her head softly toward her daughter.

"We need you to go tonight," she began.

"Why? I won't leave Dad."

"Dad's the one that said you should go."

"How? He hasn't been awake in over a week."

"We talked months ago. When he first failed, the weekend of your first race."

Deena uncrossed her legs from underneath her and leaned toward her mom. "What did he say?"

"He wants you to live your life. He was so worried you were putting everything on hold for him. He doesn't want that."

"Maybe *I* want that," Deena chimed in, but even as she said this, she was unsure of its truth.

"And maybe you do," her mom continued smoothly. "But it would be against his wishes. Baby, it's your senior year. Next year, you'll be in college."

She trailed off and stared intently at Deena, her eyes growing larger. "College," she repeated. "College. What about college?"

Deena tried shrugging as nonchalantly as possible, as if she'd never even considered the thought of college. Mom grasped Deena's hands in her own and pulled her chair another inch closer until their knees were touching.

"You're going to college," her mom said. "We've never thought otherwise. We've just been sidetracked by . . . by . . . this." Mom waved her hand in the direction of the living room, as if her dad's cancer were a slight detour and not a massive roadblock.

Deena sensed her need to reassure her mom that she would, indeed, go to college. "OK," she said, making eye contact with her mom. "OK."

"And please go tonight, please. It would mean so much to your dad."

Deena dreaded the thought of going to the team dinner. She expected her teammates would shoot daggers at her for dropping out of the qualifying race. But it was clear what her dad wanted her to do, so she had no choice but to say, "OK, I'll go."

•   •   •

Carly's house was in North Philly, a few blocks from where Deena lived when she was a kid. The street had more potholes than pavement, and a few of the houses had clearly been abandoned. Deena approached Carly's house, which was sandwiched between an overgrown lawn on one side and a falling-down porch on the other. She stood at the end of the sidewalk and looked at the door. To Deena, the door seemed to cast a shadow, even though there was a soft, warm light coming from the ground-floor window. She could hear the laughter and chatter inside. She turned to go— she couldn't be here, it didn't seem right. Her heart was thudding in her chest.

Deena thrust her hands into her pockets and began walking away. She thought of the comfy corner chair in her home, the book waiting on the side table. Then she stopped.

No, she thought to herself, *I can't hide anymore*. She turned around on the sidewalk and walked directly up to the front door before she could talk herself out of it. She pulled open the screen door and knocked three times.

"Come in!" came a voice from inside. "It's open!"

Deena pushed her way into the small entrance. The team, Mr. Humphries, and two adults whom she recognized as Carly's parents were crowded around the kitchen table. Heaping bowls of salad and steaming casseroles of ziti lined the table. Everyone was standing, preparing to say grace.

"Hi," Deena said meekly, taking off her sneakers and placing them in the pile with everyone else's.

Carly's mom, who seemed surprised at the silence, was the one to respond. "We're so glad you're here, Deena. Come join us to say grace." She shot Carly a confused glance that seemed to say, *Move over and let her into the circle.*

Deena flashed back to the first day of practice. Everyone was looking at her crossly and whispering behind her back. She was, once again, an outsider.

Carly held firm for a second, gripping Monique's hand to her right, before she finally dropped her hand and stepped to the left. Deena filled the empty space and grasped her teammates' hands.

Carly's father said grace. Everyone responded with "Amen." They then started to fill their plates with spoonfuls of pasta and salad.

The conversation slowly started again, with everyone talking between mouthfuls of food. Deena looked at Mr. Humphries, who was directly across from her. His dark eyes held her gaze. He seemed to be encouraging her to speak, to say something. She shook her head slightly, dismissing whatever thought was forming in his mind. She saw him sigh and drop his eyes to his plate.

The talk turned to tomorrow's race: the State Championships. They began discussing strategy: which teams would be the most competitive, which racers had a chance to win. Still, Deena said nothing. She moved the food around her plate and followed the conversation from one speaker to the next.

There was a brief silence, broken by Monique. "You thinking about racing tomorrow?" Monique said to Deena, with obvious anger in her eyes.

Deena looked across the table at her. She was sitting to Mr. Humphries' left. She held a forkful of ziti in midair and raised her eyebrows, a challenge, when Deena met her gaze. Deena looked at the red nail polish, which was so striking against the fork's silver.

"I mean," Monique continued, "you think you'll have the time?"

Mr. Humphries put down his fork as if protesting. But he said nothing.

"Yes, I'm planning on it," Deena said, ignoring the obvious sarcasm. She didn't want to fight about anything. She didn't want to cry about anything. She didn't want to deal with anything more than having dinner with her teammates and returning home.

"How *generous* of you," Monique said, and then she leaned forward to snatch the ziti off her own fork. She set about chewing while still watching Deena.

Deena lowered her eyes and looked at the melted cheese crusted on top of her helping of ziti. She pried the cheese from the pasta and then let her fork rest on the plate's side. She felt like she was running in mud. There was no dry ground.

No one else spoke. She guessed they were expecting her response.

"I have something to say," Mr. Humphries interjected. "Not being at the city meet was Deena's decision. And it will remain her decision. But I would like to caution all of you because sometimes assuming the worst is the biggest mistake of all." He made eye contact with Deena. "And that's all I have to say," he concluded, somewhat reluctantly.

A few seconds later, Mr. Humphries placed his hands on either side of his chair and prepared to stand. "Stay," Deena said, surprising herself at the directness of the command. He heard her and sank back into his chair.

Deena took a deep breath and looked around the room, at each one of her teammates. "I'm sorry," she began. "I'm sorry I wasn't there last weekend. I'm so sorry I let everyone down. I should have talked with everyone, but I just couldn't."

She stopped here. Maybe she didn't want to say this out loud. It would be so real if she said it out loud. But it *was* real.

"My dad is sick," she said, making eye contact with Mr. Humphries for reassurance. He nodded.

"He's really sick. We weren't sure if last weekend was it, so I made the decision to stay with him." She struggled to speak her words evenly because of the sob in her throat. She repeated, "I'm so sorry," and trailed off, relieved to have spoken the words she came to say.

Carly, sitting next to her, put an arm around Deena's shoulder and pulled her close. "We had no idea," she whispered. She looked around at everyone else, hoping they would help her in this moment. "It's OK, girl," she continued. "We got your back. I promise."

Monique said nothing, but briefly put her hand on Deena's shoulder.

Before leaving Carly's house, each teammate approached Deena and hugged her. Deena kept wiping tears from her eyes, nodding as they reassured her. She knew then that she should have told everyone sooner. She had made a mistake.

Deena put on her sneakers and then stood. She was face to face with Mr. Humphries, whose eyes were glistening with emotion. He nodded slightly at her, a gesture of approval.

Deena shook her head back and forth—the movement was an apology—and then she gave her coach a hug.

"I'm proud of you," he said.

The next morning, it was raining. The bus left Ben Franklin early because it was a two-hour drive to Penn State University, host of the Pennsylvania State Championships. Deena sat in the front seat across the aisle from Mr. Humphries. Even after she'd become friends with everyone, she continued sitting in that seat. It was a tradition she didn't want to break. She liked the time to herself. But she no longer listened to music on the rides. She kept her phone next to her on the seat, keeping it fully charged.

The bus's windshield wipers whooshed back and forth, calming her nerves. The drive was long, but it passed quickly because there was so much to think about. The race, her dad, her future, potential college applications for the spring, even an upcoming test she was worried about in math class. Math had never been her strongest subject.

Deena kept her phone in her pocket on the warm-up jog around the course. It was the agreement she'd made with her mom: she'd attend the race only if her mom stayed glued to her phone and called her if anything important happened.

The day was chilly and wet, with leaves plastered across the grass. Deena buried herself in her hooded sweatshirt and camped out in the team's tent while the other classification races took place. Ben Franklin's start time was 2 p.m.

Deena began stretching about 30 minutes beforehand and then, along with her teammates, slowly made her way to the starting line. Mr.

Humphries was there to collect their warm-ups and offer last-minute advice for the race.

"Deena and Carly." He looked at the two of them for a second each. "Run together. Lock up the front of the race. You both have the speed and stamina to match anyone else. Whoever has more in the final mile, go for it."

He looked at the rest of the group and said, "We need you all. Keep these two in your sights for as long as you can, and then remember that each point will make the difference today. Run with courage—you all have it in you."

And as they did before each race, they put their hands into the middle and announced to every team around them which school they were running for.

Deena jumped up and down and stretched her calves as she always did before each race. The rain continued to fall. When it landed on her skin and the wind cut across her legs and arms, goose bumps formed. She couldn't wait to start running, if only to allow her body to warm. She was prepared for running. It would be the easiest thing she'd done in the last few weeks.

Deena and Carly strode off the starting line together as the hundreds of runners funneled into a stream of colors racing toward the first turn into the woods. The two of them ran shoulder to shoulder, often with matching strides, for the race's first mile. Nothing was said between them, only the communication of breathing and running. Their legs did all the talking.

The lead pack of eight runners, including Deena and Carly, created distance between themselves and the second pack of runners as they entered the second mile. Deena kept her eyes ahead and steadied everything about her form: her arms were tight to her chest, her legs were landing rhythmically below her. A cluster of trees, their leaves a beautiful auburn, marked the exit from the woods. Deena watched as the branches and leaves slanted sideways in the rain and wind. As they ran past, she admired the sturdy trunks. Each was planted steadily into the ground and had been for probably hundreds of years.

How dependable trees were, Deena thought to herself as they left the woods behind, *never moving or disappearing.*

The lead pack took a turn and merged onto one of the park's paved roads. Up ahead was a long, steady hill that ended about a quarter of a mile from where they were. She heard Carly whisper, "Let's attack it," and she could feel a slight increase in pace. Deena followed her lead, and the two of them leaned into the hill, churning their legs at the same speed. She did not look behind her, but she could feel that at least one, maybe two members of the lead pack had drifted behind, unable to keep pace on the hill. A few went with them and remained on their heels.

Deena and Carly knew the course from warm-ups. They'd walked the course once and jogged it a second time. The top of the hill marked the unofficial halfway mark. They would then continue straight on the back road until they caught a separate entrance into the woods. They would be in the woods for a half mile before merging into the initial path in the woods. This would then bring them into the open grassy field that also served as the starting point. On the left was a soft dirt path that led to the finish line.

Deena pictured all of this as they churned up the hill without slowing their pace. Her legs burned with the effort, and by the time the road leveled off, she was grateful for the reprieve. Both of them were breathing heavily, and it took another quarter mile before their dangerously high heart rates leveled to something manageable.

They entered the woods just a few yards ahead of the pack. Sticks crunched under their running flats. They avoided packs of slick, wet leaves, and made sure to stay away from roots protruding from the ground. In part, races through woods were obstacle courses. But Deena was always grateful for the woods because they offered distraction from the repetition of a paved road.

They merged onto the initial wooded path, now just a little under a mile from the finish. Deena could hear the footsteps and breathing of the other girls behind them. She would not need to turn around for more evidence.

"Let's go," Carly whispered again, and Deena felt a further lengthening of her stride. She was grateful in that moment to Carly because, if she'd been by herself, she might have become too distracted by the pain of the hill, by the rain, by the gloom of the woods, to remember when and where to make a move. She was not yet as experienced as Carly, she understood now.

Their strides were long as they hurled themselves through the woods. Their initial burst had put some distance between them and several runners in the competing pack, but those runners had drawn closer throughout the ensuing quarter mile.

Deena rapidly sucked in air. Her heartbeat throbbed in her collarbone, which she recognized as a sure sign of working her upper limits. Despite this, she kept her eyes straight ahead and matched each of Carly's strides.

The natural shade of the woods ended a few hundred yards ahead of them. This was, Deena knew, the final stretch of the race. She stayed with Carly as they landed on the soft cushion of the path. Abruptly, the dirt and leaves switched to pavement, and they could hear the click of their running spikes against the hard surface. Within three strides, they were on the grass.

Deena's leg muscles faltered, exhausted from the earlier uphill push. She kept her eyes straight ahead because now they could see the finish line in the distance. It appeared on the horizon as a collection of color: people the size of tiny dots, all congregating in the general vicinity of the finish line. She thought for a second that she might have to slow down, just for a few strides, just to collect herself, but Mr. Humphries appeared in her peripheral vision. He was jogging ahead of them along the side of the course, glancing between them and his stopwatch.

"Less than two minutes left; don't worry about who's behind you," he called to them as they whizzed past. "Focus on the finish. Eyes up. Eyes ahead."

Deena felt her eyes water from the wind and exhaustion. The finish line became blurry as the water fell from her eyes and mixed with the rain and sweat.

"Time to go," Carly said.

Deena could feel the burst of speed Carly injected into her stride. She wasn't sure she possessed this gear, but she tried to go with Carly. She tried to match her stride and stay on her shoulder. She could feel her body straining with the effort. Like a race car, her body was reaching its red line. She could hear the sounds of other runners who were still close behind her.

Deena stayed on Carly's shoulder until they came off the grass and onto the final dirt straightaway. The finish line was directly in front of them, becoming larger with each step. Then Carly pulled ahead of Deena by the width of a shoulder. It happened in slow motion, because Deena would not quit on herself, but Carly put inches, and then feet between the two of them. She had more speed in those final steps.

Carly flew through the finish line. Deena came through in second place, just a stride behind. She could feel those behind her cross the finish line within seconds afterward. They had all pushed each other beyond what each of them, individually, was capable.

Ben Franklin High School finished second— the best finish in school history at the state championship meet.

Deena began walking toward the tent almost as soon as she finished the race. She hugged Carly and then continued on because she needed to check her phone. She wouldn't let her family down. She walked gingerly—her muscles depleted of energy—back to the tent, meekly thanking anyone congratulating her as she passed.

She fished her phone out of the side pocket of her backpack and illuminated the screen. There were no new messages. Finally, she bent over her legs and allowed herself a moment of happiness.

"Deena," Mr. Humphries seemed out of breath when he found her. "Where'd you go?

There's someone here I'd like you to meet."

She raised the phone to show Mr. Humphries why she'd left so quickly. His face dropped. "Is everything OK?"

"Everything is OK."

Mr. Humphries turned and waved. A small, athletic-looking black woman walked over and stood next to him. She wore a tracksuit. In small print above its right chest were the words "Shippensburg University."

"Coach White, this is Deena Jackson."

Mr. Humphries turned to Deena, a gleam in his eye.

"Deena Jackson, this is Coach White, head coach at Shippensburg University."

Coach White extended her hand, and Deena leaned forward to meet her halfway.

Chapter 8

Deena's father died in their living room with his wife and children gathered around his hospital bed. They had been lucky, if you can call it that, because they knew the end was coming. Each had time to say a special goodbye, even if it was only holding his hand for an hour without anyone else in the room.

Dad had asked to be taken off any machine helping to keep him alive, including all medications except the morphine that made his pain bearable. The doctors and nurses explained that the cancer had been one of the most aggressive they'd ever seen. That week in late summer had been the eye of the storm, the final breather before the real forces attacked.

In the early morning, Dad slipped away. Deena was standing behind her mother, who was seated at her husband's side. Jamal, with tears in his eyes, had been sitting on the other side, gripping his father's other hand.

Deena had had an hour with Dad only the night before. He couldn't say much because his strength wasn't just diminished; it was gone. She sat next to him and told him all her plans. She told him about college, her goals for running, what programs she was considering majoring in, what dreams she held for after college. Her father listened, his eyes sometimes closed, sometimes open. He blinked once, hard, and Deena took that as a sign that he approved of what she'd said. "Thank you, Daddy," she'd said, resting her forehead on his head. "Thank you for always believing in me."

The nurses had cautioned that the end would come so quietly that they might feel cheated, as if death had slipped in and out without presenting itself, without giving them a chance to fight. Deena didn't feel anything like that. She felt tears slipping down her cheeks, and she felt her mom's shoulders heaving beneath her hands. She wasn't angry at death, as they'd warned she might be. She simply missed her dad. She missed him immediately, the very second after he was gone.

The nurses made the appropriate calls, and soon Dad wasn't there in any form. For the first time in months, their living room contained only the couch and the TV.

Exhausted and bleary-eyed, her mom excused herself and went to bed. Deena followed her down the hall and climbed into her own bed, still wearing her jeans, sweater, and shoes. She fell asleep for long enough that when she awoke, the morning sun was streaming through her window. It was a crushing blow when she remembered that her dad was gone.

Deena slipped off the bed and dropped to her knees next to the bed. She put her elbows on the comforter. She closed her eyes and bowed her head. Her mind was waging its own battle: *This will never get better, you'll get through this, no you won't, yes you will, why, why, why, why, why . . .*

She lifted her head and opened her eyes. Her vision was filled with the black-and-white image of Wilma Rudolph. She admired again the steely focus of her look, the tangle of muscles in her arms and legs. And she read the poster's caption: "Wilma Rudolph, the world's fastest woman, 1940–1994."

Her dad now had two dates next to his name, too. But while he had been alive, he'd wanted this for her. She wouldn't let him down, and he would remain forever in her heart.

Deena braced herself against the bed and stood up from her kneeling position. In the corner of the room was her overstuffed reading chair. She dropped onto its edge and reached for her sneakers. She took her time unlacing and then re-lacing the sneakers. She double-knotted the laces and pulled each one tight, ensuring they wouldn't slip loose during the run.

She was planning a long one.

Deena walked down the quiet hallway and into the living room. On the coat rack hung her new warm-up jacket, with "Shippensburg University" printed across the chest.

She zipped the jacket to her chin before stepping into the cold.